HIGHLAND
FALLS

†

HIGHLAND FALLS

†

BY BLAG DAHLIA

RARE BIRD
LOS ANGELES, CALIF.

THIS IS A GENUINE RARE BIRD BOOK

Rare Bird Books
6044 North Figueroa Street
Los Angeles, CA 90042
rarebirdbooks.com

FIRST TRADE PAPERBACK ORIGINAL EDITION

Cover Art by Zoe Lacchei
Design by Dana Collins

Set in Baskerville
Printed in the United States

10 9 8 7 6 5 4 3 2 1

Library of Congress Control Number: 2021951759

Publisher's Cataloging-in-Publication Data available upon request.

To laugh means to be malicious, but with a good conscience.

—*Nietzsche*

{ 1 }

Pop Tarts
and Limousines

†

NINA WEST RODE A BICYCLE IN SPITE OF the virtues of physical fitness. Though to drive was the dream of every suburban something-year-old, she preferred to pedal or hitchhike as the mood struck her. It was a mood that changed as often and as maddeningly as the definition of virtue itself. The moment she treasured most was returning home, setting her things down and basking in the delicious warmth of solitude. After three minutes of this she'd get bored. Masturbation was too easy, but often she did it anyway.

With three blocks to go and visions of blueberry pop tarts in her head a long black limousine sideswiped the bicycle knocking Nina to the ground. In the blackness behind her eyes entire universes were created, matured and collapsed; she worked out a unified field theory in physics and hit upon a way to make the United States Congress function rationally, then awoke to a pair of concerned brown eyes set beneath a pompadour shellacked with product until its rigid glory purred—*"tease me."*

No stranger to a warm backseat, Nina came to her senses as the limo glided through darkening streets without regard for dogs or pedestrians, the driver cursing in a guttural Spanish.

"Where am I?"

"You had an accident, young lady, most unfortunate. But we are rushing to see that you get excellent medical attention immediately."

She heard the mock concern in that honey dripping voice, sensed the faux sincerity in those eyes even as she noted Highland Hospital receding in the rearview mirror. She wondered if this was an abduction and how the kidnappers could possibly be this cute, an alluring scent wafting from her seat mate's smoothly shaven face, his suit so impeccably tailored he could have wandered in off the set of a telenovela. A few blocks later, undeterred by a flashing red light blinking in the intersection the driver pulled into a hidden driveway, entered a passcode and descended into an underground parking garage.

"Where are you taking me?" asked Nina, her voice steady. These guys just didn't seem like criminals, more like international frat boys out for a night on the town. The driver parked and then sprang from the car running full speed for the elevator. The gentleman in the back exited gracefully, then turned and offered his hand to Nina as she got out.

"Where are my manners? I was so very concerned with your wellbeing that I have forgotten to introduce myself. Fernando de Gaspara at your service. And you are?"

"I'm Nina and my head hurts."

She chomped her teeth together a couple of times to complete the joke, but Fernando didn't get it. Ascending in the elevator they arrived at a luxurious suite of offices where a kindly man in hospital scrubs said-

"Buenos dias, Senorita, I am Dr. Bulbon. Have a seat here and follow the beam of my flashlight with your eyes please."

After thirty minutes of testing to determine the extent of Nina's injuries, the doctor pronounced her perfectly healthy and made a quick exit along with the visibly relieved driver. Nina wondered why she hadn't been asked to remove her clothes for the examination; not that there was any practical reason to, but it might have been fun.

"Miss West, it appears that your unfortunate mishap has left you none the lesser and for that I am overjoyed. Won't you join me for supper?"

"Where are we exactly?"

"Forgive me, you are a guest of the Bolivian Embassy of Greater Chicago, Highland Falls Annex. And the chef here makes a fine lomo montado, I can assure you."

The lomo was indeed fine, as was the ceviche, while the dulce de membrillo was just a tad quince heavy. Relaxing over drinks in the library with its mahogany paneling and twenty-foot arched ceiling, Nina ruminated on what exactly these Bolivians had done to get exiled from Chicago proper to the posh hinterlands of Highland Falls. No doubt it involved something shady with just a hint of nepotism and a *soupcon* of stupidity. She felt one of her little moments start to come on and welcomed the distraction. These spells, a mild form of epilepsy, had concerned her late parents greatly, but Nina reasoned it was better than having the writhing-on-the-floor-with-a-spoon-in-your-mouth variety. By this point, she even enjoyed these little vacations from reality, they seemed to disorient everyone except herself.

"Miss West, are you feeling all right? Would you like to lie down a moment?"

The Bolivian took her in his arms then and carried her to a divan, slightly more legitimate concern now spreading over his attractive features. Nina woke from her reverie kissing him full on the mouth and grabbed at his cock. By the time they reached the sofa de Gaspara had come in his pants and apologized profusely for it, first in Spanish and then English. Nina struggled to keep from laughing while Fernando appeared to shrink in his now somewhat more peccable suit.

"You half-baked aristocrats almost killed me with your car, then instead of taking me to a hospital you took me here just to cover your ass. Now, when I want to fuck you can't even do that right. Maybe it's time you thought about how to get on my good side, Señor Greasy Drawers."

Nina was not smiling as she delivered the rebuke, she rarely did. Men lying or scheming or obsessing at least piqued her morbid curiosity, but premature creamers just made her angry. De Gaspara liked to say that he hated America, but loved American women. This was the side of them he could do without. Maintaining hope that a mutually satisfying arrangement could still be made that didn't involve an international incident or his uncle Alejandro's private militia, he asked- "How can I be of service to you, Ms. West?

{ 2 }

A Fatal
Mistake

✝

RICKY AWOKE IN HIS PARENTS' BED, NOW HIS.

The unassuming suburban house was just fourteen hundred square feet, no waterfall or marble hot tub included. Still, to Ricky it was Buckingham Palace and he intended to celebrate here for the rest of his life. No more roommates or landlords, no more car wash, pizzeria or retail sales. And no more Allison. Ricky Lee was free to come and go as he pleased, free to say and do whatever he wanted. The best part was he had nowhere to go and nothing to say. All that was left was the funeral at a mortuary just around the corner from his parents' house, now his.

Ricky didn't like to walk nor was he partial to bicycles. Motorcycles scared him, as did scooters, skateboards and public transportation. Rather than trudge those three hundred agonizing yards through the Mecklenburgs' hedges, he got in his late mother's Honda mini-van and drove around the block, coming to rest in front of the High-land Falls Funeral Home.

"God has given, God has taken away, blessed be…"

Ricky was not a sentimental person. He couldn't remember the last time he had cried. It might have been during a particularly emotional episode of *Buffy the Vampire Slayer*. He had always loved his mother Doris Leiber and his father Morris Leiber; their passing had not changed that, but at the news of their demise he had felt a mysterious lightness, a general feeling that everything was going to be A-OK. They had lived, mated and died together and now they were no more. Ricky didn't know if he was sad or just jealous of them.

"...loving father, enthusiastic watcher of birds...devoted mother and collector of porcelain figurines..."

Ricky's eyes wandered to the ceiling. He thought about the 77" screen on what was now his Sony HD TV; about the remote control and how his father had let its battery go dead. That sort of thing wouldn't happen on his watch.

It was then that Ricky made the fatal mistake of wanting: black hair, white face, turned up nose and an outfit that looked like Wednesday Addams assaulting Jackie O outside a roller rink in 1982. In chronological terms she could have been his niece, his daughter or even his granddaughter had this been Southern Illinois, but her eyes marked her as a soul far older than he. To say that for Ricky the world stopped turning on its axis and the stars winked jubilantly in their heavens would not have been an overstatement. His parent's mortality forgotten, he felt his penis harden and slice into the zipper holding together the pants of his only suit.

It had been so long since Ricky had had an erection he thought he'd forgotten how. An insistent tumescence like this one was practically a high school relic. He felt a surge of power course through his veins. Though his forebears were dead, Ricky Lee felt very much alive now that this perfect female and he both inhabited Highland Falls and for the first time in his life Ricky Lee fell uncombed head over unfashionable heels in love, there was no other word for it. Blood evacuated his brain, briefly visiting his heart before settling at the tip of his cock. His head began to swim and he felt the urge to stand and declare his undying devotion to this woman right here in front of what remained of Morrie's Scrabble partners and Dorrie's bridge circle. If he could make this one dream come true there might be hope for him yet. He rose to his feet raising his right hand and passed out, collapsing in a heap on the parquet floor.

That cut the service short. Concerned family friends surrounded him and eventually he found himself in a small room with a stained glass window on a little cot where he promptly fell asleep. He dreamed dreams of indolence and foreboding; of paperweights and the Magna Carta; of death and Thai food in little white boxes; all things mundane, sublime, pedestrian and magnificent. In repose, Ricky Lee projected himself out across the infinite void until he could see and experience all things simultaneously, a being of pure energy and radiance returning to the bosom of the community that had spawned him. His family gone, he smiled as he slept and dreamed of a proud bird soaring, nest attached to its underside like a home away from home. He awoke feeling refreshed and confident. Sleep had done him good, it always did. The world was his oyster and every month had an "R" in it. As he rose to his feet the lights went out.

"Hey, I'm still here. Jesus!"

When the lights came on again that weirdly attractive young woman was regarding him like a Chinese dockworker regarding mullet dumped on a warehouse floor. Her workday had come to an end and she was determined to lock up and set the alarm, not babysit the bereaved.

"Can I help you with something, Woody...."

Ricky realized too late after standing that his penis had lost none of its earlier hardness. This unexpected conversation with she-who-had-made-him-rediscover-his-genitals only added to his excitement and mortification. He thought of what it would feel like to be inside her.

"It's Ricky, Ricky Lee. Well, Leiber actually, I'm here for the funeral service of my parents Morris and..."

"The party's over, Mr. Lee, the bells have been rung, the tears shed, there's nothing left to do now but get on with the business of living."

As she said this she deftly maneuvered him through a marble foyer and onto the sun porch where, after setting the alarm and triple locking the door, she motioned for him to hurry up and get downstairs before she really got impatient. Ricky instinctively paused, feeling humiliated and angry, but when he started to say something the girl held an open palm up and asked him which way he was headed. Caught short at this first hint of humanity, he motioned to the left and gave a kind of awkward bow. The girl turned to the right, padding off around the building to a basement entrance on the side, her posture erect in the gathering twilight.

{ 3 }

Death Be
Not Smart

✝

THE HIGHLAND FALLS FUNERAL HOME WAS a genuine community landmark. Established in 1947 by Fredo Minarini, the quality of service had remained high decade after decade despite all of the wars, recessions and riots the rest of the country had endured. Grandpa Minarini, well past retirement age, had hoped that one of his sons might someday run the family business. When that didn't pan out he had pinned his hopes on grandson Angelo "Ace" Minarini. Ace had flunked out of Highland High a functional illiterate, but took the mantle on, insisting only that his band the Dunderhearts be allowed to rehearse in the Home's enormous soundproofed basement amid the formaldehyde and corpses. The office work he left to his youthful, industrious girlfriend who excelled at it.

"1-2-3-4…"

This represented the sum total of Ace's knowledge of mathematics, but it had helped to win him, if not the heart, then at least the pert breasts and firm bottom of Nina West, several years his junior and in all other respects his infinite superior. She wasn't a fan of loud music, or of music in general, content to listen to whatever happened to be on television. But there was something about young dudes in a basement sweating and screaming that made her want to fuck. When the song (indistinguishable from the one before it) was over Ace walked to where Nina stood, large plugs in both her ears, and kissed her like a hyena masticating a lion cub. He grabbed a warm bottle from the top of an amplifier and drained it, coming tantalizingly close to the wet cigarette butt floating at the bottom.

"Light up that weed, fool!"

While Nina was confident that this wouldn't make the Dunderhearts play any better, she was equally sure it wouldn't make them any worse. Either way, what did it matter? Beethoven had long since rolled over.

"Hey, aren't you supposed to put the bodies away before we rehearse?"

Birdie poked at the hardening arm of Edward Johannes, dead of complications from pneumonia. Birdie was the only one among them who read books without pictures and spoke in complete sentences. He played the guitar and sang back up passably well, but his nickname came from the wide-eyed expression of terminal surprise he donned when intoxicated.

"Don't touch him, asshole! He's not a mannequin."

He mispronounced it "*mannaquinn*" and Nina laughed in Ace's face, something she did so frequently he mistook it for affection. Nina did indeed like Ace, not just for what he was, but for what he wasn't. He wasn't ever going to tell her what to do because he really didn't care one way or the other, at least in front of his friends. And though he was dumb, he was smart enough to know it would never last between them a second longer than she wanted it to.

"It creeps me out having them so close to the grow room."

It was Birdie who had come up with the idea of cooking meth in the Home's basement after binging on *Breaking Bad* reruns. With its pre-existing chemical smells, top-notch ventilation system and legitimate business cover it seemed ideal, but though his intentions were pure Birdie was a second-rate chemist. There was an explosion and a fire and afterwards it stank so badly that even the corpses smelled like cat piss. The speed idea was abandoned and they started growing very average marijuana hydroponically instead.

Old Fredo never ventured into the basement anymore, having spent twenty-five years as head embalmer. Two days a week he came into the office to review the books; otherwise he played bocce while a few trusted daytime employees, and now Nina, did all the real work. Grandson Ace's role was largely symbolic, but he did perform one indispensable function, transporting the newly dead from the scene of their final reckoning to the Highland Falls Funeral Home via the family hearse.

Auto accidents, natural disasters, suicides; Ace was responsible for conveying the kind of mishaps that make a mess, but don't require an autopsy. He was surprisingly good at it, too, discrete in a take-charge sort of way that put the victim's family, the paramedics and even the Illinois State Police at ease. When he arrived at the scene of a tragedy clad in white shirt and tie, senseless mayhem seemed almost sensible. When it came to honest work of any kind though, his black shriveled heart just wasn't in it. Ace Minarini, born without talent, was born to rock.

"1-2-3-4!"

Nina disappeared up the stairs and out the front door. A limousine pulled in front of the Home and five young men in identical black suits got out, suspicious bulges clearly visible under their jackets. They each carried two large diplomatic pouches from the Bolivian Embassy. Nina met them on the steps, received the packages without a thank you and, like a more attractive Noah, loaded them two by two into the Highland Falls Funeral Home.

{ 4 }

Sticky
Modern
Problems

✝

IT HAD BEEN FOUR YEARS SINCE RICKY had last made the pilgrimage home and he hoped that nostalgia would give way in time to contentment. Fortunately, any friends he had in Highland Falls were long gone. Entering the master bedroom, he felt the soft carpet beneath his feet. Heading into the bathroom, he let loose a great whooshing flood of hot water and when the tub filled he soaked in it, a rape shower for the unambitious. He threw in the last of his mother's blueberry oatmeal bubble bath and felt it froth between his toes. He remembered the girl from the funeral, the bitchy one, and his cock began to grow.

Watching the Nature channel, the cycle of birth/death/rebirth had always left him vaguely unsatisfied. A surprise baby himself with no siblings and no offspring to call his own, the buck that was the Leiber dynasty stopped with Ricky Lee. Trapped between eternal teenhood and a disappointing adulthood he had always surfed the very edge of uselessness, toiling little, accomplishing nothing. Allison, with her anti-anxiety pills and guided meditations, heard the sound of one hand clapping and repeatedly walked out on him. Well, this time it was his turn.

Floating in the tepid tub his cock swelled for the last of a dying breed, pointing grandly toward the vaulted ceiling. You never saw one of those in a rented flat, or lounged in a clean tub without decades of strangers' feet beneath you, for that matter. After bathing, he inspected the medicine cabinet and shelves. He shaved, flossed, trimmed, and then even moisturized for the first time. It couldn't hurt, right? And it was free.

He slept, awoke, then napped. When he opened his eyes again, Ricky looked up through the skylight that arched above his parent's bed, now his. The sky was a poor substitute for what he really wanted as he pawed at the remote control. Soon a glow spread across the room and two vaguely rural figures kissed and caressed each other until a semi-truck brought their whole boudoir crashing down around them to the dulcet strains of banjo music. You could almost smell the muscle car fumes as the Duke Boys, ancient masculine artifacts of a time long past, pulled up to save the day.

As afternoon shadows grew longer, pirates sailed soldiers grimaced models pranced Indian chiefs made war and technology solved sticky modern problems; jungles teemed caverns yawned cities seethed suburbs undulated and farm folk tilled, the salt of the Earth. Ricky's hands wandered toward his crotch with no remorse. By sheer attrition he was now a part of that great cycle of life that ends in a Kleenex sodden and torn. When he had come, he farted, and then slept again. While he slept he dreamed which qualified as free movies with no cable box required. For the next five days, twelve hours of sack time per diem guaranteed sound mental health. He not only slept, but ate and even considered excreting in bed. By her presence beside him Allison had, in a very real sense, taken *bed* away from him and for that he could never forgive her. Now, sleep and dreams had been restored to Ricky Lee and he dreamed of that nasty young girl from the funeral parlor.

{ 5 }

Enter The Kaptain

✝

IT WAS THE BEST OF TIMES, IT WAS THE best of times, and it was even better than that. Five days so blissful Ricky would never forget them. Five days so tranquil they floated like ether in halothane. Five days when no one who wasn't him mattered. A less seasoned sloth might have thought *"Fuck the World,"* but Ricky knew that would be too much effort. It all came down to my bed in my house in my country 'tis of me.

Awaking on day number six with a sense of foreboding he cried one last time for Doris and Morris. They had loved him and now they were gone. He was lost and alone and he had no one. He cried for his fears, he cried for his loneliness, but most of all he cried for himself. He wailed for the teat he would never suckle again, for the block his old chip had come off of, and the more he cried the harder the tears came, great heaving sobs and fitful gasps of air, punctuated by gentle pathetic burblings and plaintive wails of misery. He started to grow alarmed at the depth of his own emotion, the torrent of feeling that welled from within and agitated his troubled psyche. He began to hyperventilate for the times that his breath had been bad his bank account empty his dick soft his paint peeling his toilet running his life an absolute sham.

He stared at the ceiling for answers as tears poured down his face. *Where was he going? What would he do? Why had they left him all alone?*

Snot trailed from his nose toward the carpet like silly putty from a broken egg. And then he stopped sobbing. They had left him this house, that's what they'd left him. Three spacious bedrooms upstairs; guest, living and dining rooms down; well-appointed kitchen, handy laundry room and three-car-garage. He wouldn't need a bus pass anymore, not with the functional minivan and the sporty Lexus at his disposal. There was even an ancient ice cream truck Morris had bought and refurbished over Doris's strenuous objections.

His father, a lifetime company man, had always dreamed of being an entrepreneur and franchising a fleet of such trucks to service sporting events, music festivals and bar mitzvahs. The fleet never quite materialized, but aside from that one lapse in judgment, Morris and Doris appeared quite well off. Ricky had already let some mail pile up concerning checking and savings accounts, investments, loans, annuities, the whole nine yards. And, of course, there was still that pile of petty cash nestled in the same spot he used to steal it from back in high school.

It had been lean years for Ricky since he'd been booted from home. He had worked a succession of repetitive menial jobs ever since. Having now mastered deprivation and sloth, he could live off that petty cash for months before delving into the thicket of parental finances he hoped a high school education and a few PBS retirement specials had prepared him to navigate.

With that revivifying thought, he reached for the Kaptain, a sixteen-inch water pipe in the shape of a human skull that changed colors as it filled with smoke. His love affair with the Kaptain had started senior year, when a semester of Ceramics, Metal Shop, Acting and Macramé left him plenty of time to indulge. Of course, back then the weed was thirty dollars an ounce and you almost had to smoke that much to catch a buzz. Pot freaked him out now that it was cripplingly potent and had brand names like *Gorilla Biscuits* and *Fu Manchu*. He remembered trying to buy his first bag downtown in Grant Park and getting burned for ten dollars by a guy in a ratty brown sweater with one free floating eye. When he and his friends had tried to smoke the stuff it tasted like hay held together with Elmer's glue. That was when he'd realized that the city and the suburbs were two different animals. He stuck to Highland Falls after that, with zero interest in the exploration of Gotham Jr.

He would fill the Kaptain with clean water and ice and take three giant hits before breakfast, that way his mom would get used to his eyes looking red and it wouldn't raise any suspicions. Classes passed in a blur of disinterest and crib notes until he graduated from Highland High near the middle of his class. From then on, The Kaptain had been his constant companion through two and a half years away at college. It had also accompanied his ignominious return home for those three long years that passed before his parents ejected him from the nest for the rest of their natural lives.

Returning from college the Prodigal Only Child, disgraced recipient of academic expulsion from a party school, he became just useful enough not to get thrown out of the house; staggering forward, surrendering to fate. He almost became self-sufficient, learning to prepare meals using only the microwave and things that could be purchased at 7-Eleven. He did his own laundry and ironing, meaning his clothes smelled and had wrinkles. He learned to keep his mouth shut concerning politics, art and even other people's behavior. That last one was the hardest, but no one ever said surrender was easy. Finally, when Doris and Morris could stand it no longer, Ricky got the old heave-ho. Still, the Kaptain never let him down. He took a hit and held it just as long as he could.

{6}

The Road
Less Traveled

†

WHILE IT'S NEVER BEEN CLINICALLY PROVEN that playing Rock & Roll music makes you stupid, not playing it can't help but make you smarter. Even those traversing a road less traveled avoid placing their lips over the exhaust pipe. Still, to tell Ace, Birdie, Lex and Easy that they were doing irreparable damage to their ears, noses, throats and central nervous systems would have been a fool's errand.

The Dunderhearts had yet to play an actual show, but they had discussed at length how cool all the bands they liked were and how god-awful every other band was, especially the bands that everyone else liked. These conversations became more or less animated depending on how drunk they were and how late at night they happened. While everyone in the group had an opinion on everything, musically it was only Lex that really deserved one. Birdie kept his thoughts to himself and Easy just sort of chimed in nonsensically when the mood struck him. In the end, no matter what happened Ace always demanded it be his way or the highway.

Nina came downstairs bearing a silver tea tray covered in neatly chopped lines of cocaine. Upon her arrival, time stood still for the Dunderhearts and all conversation ceased as they nose fed like ants at a picnic. Real money is scarce in the Rock & Roll business and unlike a large pepperoni pizza, few rockers can actually feed a family of four. Cocaine is a universal currency though. Specifically, free cocaine because it smells better than any other kind. Though it might call to mind pink limousines and palatial hotel suites with Mick and Keith banging super models and thumbing their powdery noses at the Man, the reality was more prosaic. In this profession where each individual player is almost certainly doomed to failure, coke represented the off chance that if you burned every bridge behind you, someday you just might make it. Free cocaine is a kind of victory and musicians take their sad little victories where they find them.

"Nina, I love you."

So said Ace Minarini grinning like the feral cat who swallowed the numbingly addictive canary. Nina ignored the comment and passed the tray to Lex. He was the best looking one in the group and the most talented, stroking the neck fluidly, but with authority and playing equally well with fingers or pick. He could transpose on the spot, follow improvised changes with ease and play with equal dexterity any top 40 hit, thrash metal opus or obscure reggae drop.

Sadly, his steady job was with an ABBA cover band called Bjorn Free. In the realm of the Dunderhearts he was maligned, ignored and pitied in equal measure. Nothing infuriates a budding rock band as much as looks and talent, especially from one of their own, and a Dunderheart with a paying gig was intolerable. Nina couldn't help but be impressed by Lex's imposing seventy-five-inch frame, his flowing locks and lantern jaw, his tattooed biceps and the outline of what looked to be an enormous cock nestled in his stylish trousers. She knew that eventually they would fuck and she knew that it would be good and she knew that Ace would get mad and blame Lex for the whole sordid affair. That was half the fun. The other half was making him wait for it, possibly forever.

Next to stick his nose in the trough was Eric Abelard, aka Easy. A serviceable drummer, his real interest lay in breaking every taboo, crossing every line and pissing up every rope he ever came across. Decadent was too mild a term for this nineteen-year-old who slept in the back of his car and once fucked a quadriplegic to win a twenty dollar bet. He was the only one among them who hadn't grown up in Highland Falls at all, but seemed to have just dropped from the sky like guano from an albatross. He snorted one line, then immediately took two more before Ace grabbed for the tray sending it hurtling to the floor in an avalanche of white and silver.

"Goddamn you, motherfucker!"

Ace had his hands around Easy's throat and Nina remembered why she liked him. Perhaps, she thought, Ace will kill Easy and later she could visit him in jail. Not more than once though. Ace began grinding Easy's face into the carpet where the coke was strewn and screaming-

"You want it so bad, suck it up, asshole, have it all!"

Lex, already high and glad the abuse wasn't directed toward him, looked at Nina and detected a faint chuckle behind her perpetual scowl. Birdie moved to calm things down the only way he knew, by holding a joint under Ace's nose until he loosened his grip. Easy, face frozen and covered in powder, nose bleeding and blindingly high from his gluttony, felt the heart race in his chest. He would kill Ace, join a monastery and raise sheep in New Zealand. He would go back to school, study ornithology and stab Ace in the groin thirty-one times. He would renounce drugs, get straight, torture Ace in the basement of a slaughterhouse and run for public office as a Libertarian. Lex handed Easy a beer and he held it to his face, unable to feel its coolness. He would purchase an assault rifle at a gun show and murder Ace and everyone who had ever done him wrong. On second thought, he might try beekeeping.

"There's plenty more, guys, knock yourselves out."

Nina pulled out a brick of compressed white powder and calmly scraped some onto the platter with an X-Acto knife.

"Jesus Christ! This shit tastes like it's never been cut! You've got, like, twenty-five grand worth of raw blow here!"

Indeed, she did. And she'd already hidden the other nineteen kilos in the body storage refrigerator.

{ 7 }

Blue Marbles, Yellow Sea

†

"RICKY! RICKY LEIBER! YOU FUCKING FREAK!"

Ricky heard a familiar voice from the gutter. Thirty-one years had passed since he had last seen Feet, but their bond was as strong as ever, that is to say nonexistent. Freshman Ricky had bought weed off senior Feet a few times, nothing more. By the time Ricky graduated, Feet was already hanging out at the Dairy Queen parking lot selling pills he scrounged from between his mom's seat cushions. It appeared that he'd been consigned to the outskirts of Mount Highland where the bars, outlawed by zoning everywhere else in Highland Township, were clustered among drive-thru fast food, liquor stores and gas stations.

"Hey, Feet."

"It's Francis, man, Francis Federline. That's my name."

Ricky took a good look at Feet and involuntarily blurted-

"What the fuck?"

Feet was perched atop a wooden shelf fixed to a skateboard, but he had no lower legs to speak of, just thighs cut off above the knee. The kneepads he wore made him look like an overgrown peewee footballer wobbling toward the goal line of his next drink. Though he smelled strongly of decay his face had the same inquisitive, jolly expression it had had three decades ago, but by now there was no one left behind those eyes like blue marbles adrift on a yellow sea.

"Fuck man, I knew it was you, I knew it was you. You got a smoke?"

Ricky instinctively patted his upper and lower pockets, the international semaphore for *no cigarettes* when he felt a bump in the inside pocket of his windbreaker and pulled out Morris Leiber's last imported cigar, partially smoked. He ceremoniously handed it to Feet as a parting gesture, but it prompted another round of questions. Did he have a light, did he have any cash, did he want to get a drink at the Night'n'Gale or maybe Maggorio's Pub? Ricky was usually a one beer guy, maybe one wine if he was on a date, which was never. Booze didn't really turn him on since he'd hit the road selling t-shirts for a rockabilly band and tried unsuccessfully to imitate their wake and barf regimen. It took about a week before he realized his liver couldn't handle a career in music merchandising. For his part, Feet had reached a point in life where he was always half awake, but never fully conscious. He oozed a swampy funk out of every pore.

Maggorio's Pub had played host to the most ambition averse citizens of greater Highland Township for thirty-four years. The taps held domestic beer at bargain prices while the kitchen made chicken wings and fries served on paper plates garnished with iceberg lettuce and barbecue sauce. There was a pool table and a dartboard and the obligatory sixteen-inch softball team, *Maggorio's Mudsharks*, named after an old Frank Zappa song. Like Ricky Leiber himself, nothing on the inside of Maggorio's had changed in years.

Feet wheeled himself in and headed straight for the back door, open to keep air circulating. He laid out a folding chair and table left there by management as a compromise so he could enjoy a drink without making the other customers gag. Ricky approached the bar to order two beers and recognized three guys from a tenth grade Woodworking class as well as Bonnie Naylor and Ronnie Marquette, still making out passionately just as they had in the hallways of Highland High all those decades ago.

In his mind's eye, Ricky suddenly saw a vision of Allison dressed in a nice outfit, her hair done up and a big smile on her face as she prepared to suck another man's dick. He shook his head to lose the image, but it was too late. He had to speak to her, at least hear her voice to be sure it was just his imagination running away with him. Was there a pay phone here, he wondered? Were there any of those left anymore? Ricky felt like the last person alive who didn't have a smart phone, but amid the relentless crush of modernity he had thus far resisted the siren call of technology and didn't want to give in now that total indolence seemed finally within his grasp. He was old, he was lazy and he missed Allison.

"You got any good pills, Ricky? I don't shoot anymore since my accident, but I'll eat the fuck out of some pills."

Ricky was just formulating a reply when Feet hopped off of his chair onto his skateboard and wheeled out the back door faster than Ricky thought possible. As he turned to see what had spooked Feet he felt two strong hands around his throat lifting him out of his chair. He levitated through a power not his own, legs flailing like a spider, arms reaching out for the void. A smell like sweat and old hops poured from the hot furnace of hate that held him, then sent him crashing across the table and halfway through the back door. Given the loss of control over his own body, Ricky felt surprisingly good for just a moment, alive for the first time in recent memory, like a creature in motion on the open sea, a jellyfish shanghaied by the unyielding current and deposited he-knew-not-where.

"Don't kill him, Ronnie! I love you baby, please!"

Those were the last words that Ricky heard as Ronnie Marquette picked him up off the ground, spun him around and punched him squarely on the chin. He could not feel the back of his head hit the floor first, vibrating elliptically on rubbered neck for a moment before everything inside it went dark. Like a free bird, Ricky dreamed on.

{ 8 }

Doctor's Hospice

✝

LEAVING THE BAND FLAILING AWAY in the basement, Nina headed upstairs toward a suite of comfortable offices. Though she was a high school dropout, part-time employment gave structure to her carefree existence, but not too much. The day's work done, pleasantly high and lounging in a plush leather chair, she turned on the television and cycled through options. The news was a non-starter. Who cared about politicians, celebrities and inspiring people anyway? She wasn't optimistic enough to vote and had no interest in entertainment.

She found the music video channel insufferable. Any singing, dancing, female near her age paraded around in maddening pastel, overly white teeth bleached clean to hide the effects of bulimia. During interviews they spewed mindless chatter about what boy band star they were dating or gushed about their pathetic experiments with rudimentary lesbianism. They probably couldn't even just lay there correctly. Sports was OK, but she had never played one, didn't know the rules of any and certainly didn't give a damn which side prevailed. Anyway, in competition there were always far more losers than winners. Skipping over the Weather Channel, she flipped through the newest rom-coms, thrillers and docudramas, each more ludicrous than the next. Was everyone in Hollywood a moron or did they simply know their audience far too well?

She arrived finally at the Soap Opera channel and felt cleansed. She hadn't missed an episode of *Doctor's Hospice* since age seven, and there, in all of his curative glory, stood Dr. Lukas Cosgrove, MD. The look of genuine concern and self-confidence he radiated made her wet and her hands traveled through her panties like an ocean liner through a hot tub.

She switched the sound off the TV and turned to her phone. Nina enjoyed the internet because there was so much sex on it. True, the news and information on there was dubiously sourced, mean spirited drivel, but the sheer omnibus of perversion on offer remained too tantalizing to ignore. Social media especially afforded her a chance to let her nihilism run wild. Any snapshot she posted yielded a torrent of pathetic solicitations from rejects begging for her attention. They offered jewelry, vacations, automobiles, yet Nina never relented, never showed them an ounce of respect. To meet them in person would destroy the supremacy that online anonymity gave her, so she fought them on the digital terrain where anything goes and everybody went.

> @gerry
> OMG! You look just like that girl from the Addams Family!

> @NinisNV
> WTF! You look like a sad old guy who drives a bus in Kankakee!

> @BeavHunt420
> Your fuckin' hot! Meat at Scores by the airport, drinks on me. Lap Dance!!!

> @NinisNV
> By the airport? Did you just fly in from Somalia? I wouldn't meet you anywhere except in a jury box sentencing you to die.

> @BigDick55
> What are you wearing?

> @NinisNV
> A knowing smirk. And everyone knows you have a tiny Li'lDick55.

But it was through ambiguous innuendo that Nina really came to master the internet and its trolls. The frustration she could engender with a few tantalizing pictures and nebulous statements drove more than a few would-be Romeos off the deep end as they vainly tried to pin her down in a maze of ones and zeros. Her aim was less to catch a predator than to drive them to distraction.

> **@EddieNewport**
> RU coming over or what? There's a whole shitload of this stuff now, you still want it?

> **@NinisNV**
> OMG Eddie, that sounds bitchin'! Can you get more? Are you gonna be around this weekend at all?

> **@EddieNewport**
> Yeah, I already told you, I'm here on the boat. Still here. Wanna hang out, but I got to pay for this stuff and there's Harbor Patrol around.

> **@NinisNV**
> Totes! Here's a pic of me sunbathing and thinking about sailing. Can you get more stuff? All my friends want like 20 hits each and some tweek, too, and something to smoke.

> **@EddieNewport**
> RU and the hotties coming out here now or what?

> **@NinisNV**
> What? Hey, Jenny got a beer bong! We're getting f-ing wrecked, yo! When are you guys coming over?

And so on, until any reasonable person would roll themselves into a corner and weep softly for literacy in our day. To Nina, the thought that she could infuriate, titillate, and ultimately humiliate someone she would never have to be in the same room with filled her with a dull joy. She knew it was a colossal waste of time, yet the thrill was undeniable. It gave her the fortitude to spend another day with Ace, secure in the knowledge that she wasn't even digitally faithful to him.

> **@EddieNewport**
> When are you guys coming over for reals?

> **@NinisNV**
> OMG, Eddie, I forgot I'm supposed to do the
> Eeny Meeny Bikini contest at Flannagan's tonight.
> Come down and bring your boat!

> **@EddieNewport**
> Where's Flannagan's, can I sail to it?

> **@NinisNV**
> Joliet! margarita happy hour and free
> pizza until it runs out. We go cray cray at Flanny's!

> **@EddieNewport**
> WTF, I can't sail to Joliet

> **@NinisNV**
> Suxx 2BU! Can you get more stuff?

And so on…

{9}

Signals
Crossed

†

RICKY OFTEN DREAMED OF SEX, IT WAS easier than actually doing it. He never dreamed of fashion models, strippers or porn stars, they were all too distant and inaccessible. Sometimes he dreamed of what might be possible, but even that degree of speculation held the chance of disappointment. Usually, Ricky reflected on what he had already had. He had come of age in the 1980s among the meticulously germ-free females of suburbia, sampling their wares whenever he could. His memory had mercifully eliminated the fatties, the uglies and the acne ridden. That only left top shelf masturbation fodder, mainly from his exploits circa sixteen to twenty-three when, due to his exile from Highland Falls, he began to falter with the fairer sex for well over a decade until Allison and the last few years of domestic torture had conspired to render his cocksmanship limp and uninspired.

The golden era that spurred a thousand right handed fantasies was that wildly improbable summer after senior year when Ricky had glimpsed a sexual Shangri-La. Now, unconscious on the floor of Maggorio's, he felt the past tug at his penis like a little death and he dreamed once again of that far, far better time.

Maureen was popular and smart and enjoyed all those high school activities Ricky hated: forensics and the drama department, the yearbook and school paper, the cheerleading squad and chess club.

She was small like an orphan selling matches in front of an English flower shoppe, tiny but never trifling. The slightest curve of booty jutted insouciantly behind, as did pert breasts in front. Her skin was white like fine china, eyes green, hair an Irish red dyed redder and she always smelled good even when her heart was breaking.

For his part, Ricky Leiber was neither cute nor ugly, neither smart nor dumb; neither short nor tall, fat nor skinny. He was neither jock nor preppie nor freaky death rocker nor captain of the marching band. No, Ricky was singularly, maddeningly average. For Maureen, he was perfect! She had spotted him ogling her during a volleyball game while he feigned a sprained ankle. At the end of the period he rose, struggling to hide his erection and Maureen waylaid him to a corner of the gym behind some bleachers.

"I think I know a way to make that swelling go down. Why don't we talk it over later?"

The rest of the day passed like a 787 through clouds. He was gonna fuck Maureen Kelleher! He'd fucked two girls before and both times it was pretty good, but Maureen was in a whole other league. And she was all over him like a total slut, it was unbelievable! He wanted to shout it from the rooftops, yell at the top of his lungs, "I'm gonna stick my dick in Maureen after school today!" but he knew enough to keep his mouth shut. After school, he pulled out the Kaptain and ceremoniously cleaned it. Southern Illinois U. in the fall and a bitchin' summer ahead of him. Dad pretty much let him drive the Pinto whenever he wanted and now he'd have Maureen in the passenger seat jacking him off, too!

Seven o'clock came, the doorbell rang and Mo looked perfect. Her hair was clean and crimped and he just knew she had a nice little pussy. He couldn't wait to take a look at it, to handle and possess it, to fill it with all of his hopes and dreams. Now, all these decades later he was dreaming again, on the floor of Maggorio's Pub. It was sticky down here and he felt sore all over, but they did show a hell of a movie.

"Baby...Please..."

{ 10 }

Gunfire
and Castanets

†

FOR SIX AND THREE QUARTER MINUTES NINA posted
vaguely inflammatory comments on the memorial website of a
celebrated Muslim imam. By all accounts a pious man, he had
died somewhat ironically when his private plane crashed into the
side of a building. Nina then cruised the net looking for something interesting to masturbate to. Pornography was the cus-
tomary standby, but often she found other things to occupy her
imagination. In this case, pictures of the Harrisburg, PA little
league champs of 1987. She imagined stripping the catcher, his
tiny penis proud as it glinted in the sun that shone off home plate;
soon they were rolling in the high dirt of the pitcher's mound, as
curious infielders swarmed in to take turns. In her mind's eye, she
bucked and writhed while barkers whooped, *"peanuts, get your red
hot nuts here!"* She could almost smell the ghost of Babe Ruth in
the bleachers.

In the past, Nina had toyed with the idea of participating in a gang
bang just for the sheer depravity of it, but the thought of satisfying
anyone, let alone more than one, held little true appeal for her. Even
energetic young champions from the Keystone State didn't deserve
that much of her all at once and that fantasy died in its infancy.

Surfing the net further she came across a site dedicated to grisly
Central American drug cartel murders. Her hand in her pussy, she

visualized a troop of ruthless hitmen, conscience free, a dull coldness behind their hooded eyes. They would just as soon slit her throat as fuck her, but why choose when they could do both? Decapitated bodies of nosy journalists gathered flies in the background as street urchins prepared to set them ablaze with kerosene and wooden matches. Knocked to the ground, her *chincuete* hiked up over her face, uncircumcised cocks of every length and girth prepared to stab into her as the sound of gunfire and castanets filled the air. On the spot, a band of mariachis composed a narcocorrido, immortalizing this wayward gringa's last stand. She knew that hers would be the next body immolated and so she fought to feel every grimy thrust before death, too, had its way with her...

Nina was going along well now, but before she could orgasm she tumbled to the floor; coke dusted nose bleeding, bee stung lips retching out blueberry pop-tarts, her throat raw with the effort. She lay there exhausted for a long spell as equilibrium returned, breathing deeply. Feeling the hard surface beneath her, eyeing the grand ceiling above, she resolved that these gak fueled internet fantasies would end right here and now.

Not for Nina the virtual life, examined by squads of engineers in antiseptic California high rises, only to be lapped up by adenoidal washouts too young to know what they were missing. Let the rest of her generation piss away their hours pursuing digital phantoms, she craved carbon and calcium, blood and bone. Raising her tiny fists high she pummeled the offending squawk box gleefully, loving the red that began to spurt from the fresh gash on her wrist as the blue light flickered out for good.

{11}

What Could Possibly Go Wrong?

✝

ANY THOUGHT OF MAKING MUSIC HAD disappeared up the noses of the Dunderhearts hours ago. Easy sat behind the drum kit twirling sticks and chewing on the inside of his cheeks. His nose had stopped bleeding while a visible shiner formed across both of his eyes.

"Sorry man, blow makes me crazy. I didn't mean anything by it."

Ace's apology, the first he'd offered in years, was meant sincerely. He didn't think of himself as a violent person, it was just that when people upset him his first reaction was to cause them physical harm. For Easy, time had ceased to be operative in the space between his ears. Thoughts ricocheted off each other like crabs in a tank, skittering across his consciousness. He would join the army, become a company chef and poison those who promote war and intolerance. He would master perch fishing and use his newly acquired skills to feed aboriginals in Australia's interior. Or he might just pour a chocolate milkshake down the front of his shirt and start crying.

Ace handled his drugs far better, but those parts of his mind that he regularly shut off via beer and marijuana were forced open by cocaine in a way that made him restless. He loved music, he just knew he wasn't any good at it. What he really loved were show tunes. He'd seen *High School Musical* eight times at the movies and only quit going because of the snickering of the cashiers. What the fuck did they know anyway? Someday he would write a Broadway classic and shove that success down everyone's throat. Then they would have to acknowledge him for the singular genius he really was. Until that day came, he had resigned himself to singing ninety second odes to fucking and violence replete with expletives, poor musicianship and low production value. What could possibly go wrong?

Self-reflection soon ended, ambitions passing quickly like the try-outs on *American Showstopper.* The tray glinted silver and white in the corner of his eye, another snort beckoned. Birdie had retreated to the far corner of the room pondering a life squandered. He loved all drugs, hard drugs especially, but they always made him melancholy and ashamed. His Catholic upbringing did him no favors when these episodes kicked in and he found himself sorting through the catalog of blown chances and missed opportunities that had placed him in this dingy funeral home surrounded by imbeciles with a guitar around his neck.

Ace approached with the tray reloaded and a grin like the Cheshire Cat. He tripped over an errant guitar case on the floor, did a complete somersault and landed on his feet, his smile never wavering and the coke remaining on the surface of the tray like it had been glued there. Impressed by Ace's drugged dexterity Birdie took the straw up his nose feeling a mingled disgust/enthusiasm for the South American jungle. Before he could inhale though, Easy came up from behind and snorted every last bit in a superhuman show of nasal capacity. While Birdie was almost relieved at this turn of events, Ace was moved to action. He punched Easy very hard in the throat. Gasping for air, Easy took off running, Ace in hot pursuit.

"Guys, guys," said Birdie.

"Aaahrrrrg," panted Easy, dodging behind his kit for protection.

"You fucking cock sucker," screamed Ace, knocking the ride cymbal into Easy's forehead and vaulting over the kit. Ace landed hard on a piece of hardware with no drum attached that jutted up out of the kick drum like a spike. He screamed in pain and Easy burst into a fit of convulsive laughter. Ace decided that once he could move again he would murder his drummer and replace him with a machine. Birdie finally ambled over to where Easy stood panting and Ace lay groaning and asked-

"Hey, where's Lex at?"

Ace forgot all about Easy, the drugs and even his rage as he wondered-

"Where's Nina?"

{12}

Flashbacks
and Ass Cracks

†

DORIS AND MORRIS LEIBER HAD LEFT for the movies, *Terms of Endearment,* so Ricky had the whole house to himself. Maureen and he could start in the living room, move on to the kitchen table and finish up in the basement if he wanted. It was too perfect!

When Mo arrived they exchanged pleasantries, cracked two cans of Heilemann's Old Style and found themselves on the couch with the TV on, sound off. Ricky reached over and touched her gently freckled face, brushing back her hair and catching a faint wink of insanity behind her eyes. When their lips met the kiss was long and lingering. She smelled both pretty and fecund, like a flower in the dirt. Ricky's cock stiffened as he removed her shirt and laid her down on the brown Naugahyde. His head swam with pride and desire: desire for this bright, beautiful creature and pride for having gotten her here. Out of all of the guys at school Maureen had chosen him. Ricky Leiber would now be a real player at Highland High. She tugged at his belt and he groped at her panties, thrilled at the healthy bush that greeted his fingers. Again, their lips locked and Ricky's head swam. The end of senior year was going to turn into the best summer ever.

"Hang on, one second…"

Maureen quickly wriggled out from under Ricky, his stiff cock now lodged between two couch cushions, reached in her purse and removed a pair of handcuffs with which she deftly manacled Ricky's outstretched hands. She drove her right knee into the small of his back and grabbed him by the hair so forcefully his neck almost snapped.

"Owww!"

Maureen took a swig of the Old Style and spat it into Ricky's ear.

"Have I got your attention yet?"

As she tugged on his hair, he nodded 'yes' as best he could. She wadded up her panties and stuffed them into his mouth, yanking his pants down to his ankles to make escape impossible. Subduing this desperate horny weakling gave her a kind of thrill, just not the kind she really needed.

"You want this pussy, don't you, Ricky?"

He nodded again, sure that she was psycho and he wouldn't fuck her now if she was the last crazy bitch on Earth. As always, Ricky simply didn't understand. Maureen was a girl who liked girls, but secretly. In the Highland High pecking order of the mid-1980's female homosexuals ranked somewhere between chess nerds and Special Ed. Before internet porn, if lesbians were thought of at all it was in the guise of butch gym teachers or fishy looking cafeteria monitors. In the fishbowl that was HHS the last thing Maureen wanted was to be ostracized for her peccadilloes. She had recruited Ricky for her sexual master plan not because he stood out in any way, but precisely because he did not.

"You and me are going to fuck seven pretty girls by the end of the school year and another seven by the end of the summer. I'm going to tell them one by one how madly in love I am with Ricky Leiber and they're going to help me make you mine because every girl loves a romance with a happy ending. They won't know what hit 'em until it's way too late!"

She reached into her purse again pulling out a ten-inch black latex dildo and placing it perilously close to Ricky's exposed asshole. He could sense her grinning maniacally behind his back, his face ground into the couch faintly redolent of Morrie's chronic gas. Ricky wished with all his heart that he was dead. If Maureen went through with this, if that enormous phallus penetrated him, he would have to move somewhere far away from Highland Falls and never return. She turned a switch on the dildo and it started to vibrate Ricky's perineum. He froze as time squatted still. Somewhere, Oscar Wilde in sequined vest and platform heels threw confetti with a mouth full of pubic hair. Ricky's cock was flaccid now and he swore to himself that if the experience to come gave him an erection he would have to commit suicide.

"You're going to get me some pussy, Ricky, and when I get some," here she leaned in and licked the beer residue from his ear, "you're gonna get some. And together we'll have the Best…Summer…Ever! Do we have a deal?"

With that she turned the key in the cuffs and sprang to her feet grabbing the panties from Ricky's mouth and releasing her grip on him. He struggled back into his clothes so relieved to be free he resisted the overwhelming urge to punch Mo Kelleher in her pert little upturned nose.

Ricky's mind rarely raced, it was usually content to lounge reclining, but it was at least jogging now. This bitch really was psycho and a dyke to boot. Her plan sounded crazy, fourteen chicks in fourteen weeks, they could never pull it off. He'd probably get his face slapped by a bunch of angry females, his ass kicked by irate boyfriends; maybe they would even be expelled or hauled off to the Highland Police station before it was all over. He didn't like Maureen, he didn't even like himself anymore, but he was seventeen and he did like sex.

"Deal."

{13}

Six Six Six
Thirteen

✝

"BABY...PLEASE...BABY...PLEASE..."

The words pounded through the skull of Ricky Lee on the floor of Maggorio's Pub unleashing memories of that Technicolor summer that had rendered the rest of his life a grainy black and white.

The first beauty that Maureen and Ricky debauched was Gail Blalock, chosen for her smoldering good looks and general accessibility. She had dated lacrosse hero Randy Kolchek exclusively from freshman year through his untimely demise behind the wheel of the '67 Camaro that he treasured above all things. Any amount of alcohol now put Gail in the mood and whomever happened to be around when she started drinking was in for a treat. Sharing a Bunsen burner in chemistry class, Maureen told of her unrequited crush on Ricky Leiber, that she longed to let him know how she felt, but just couldn't figure out how to hook him. What really hooked Gail was the disclosure of Ricky's possession of a fake ID and love of Boone's Farm fortified wine.

With both date and bait set it was only a matter of getting the three of them in the same room at the same time. Gail, still convinced she was merely facilitating Mo's snaring of Ricky, invited them both over to watch the finale of *M*A*S*H* on TV. They played a drinking game where every time Hawkeye took a drink they all had to. In no time, Gail was naked on all fours with Maureen's tongue exploring the inside of her pussy while Ricky shoved his cock down her throat. Ten minutes later, intoxicated by the scent of vaginal juice and faux mango alcohol, Mo experienced her first nonsolo orgasm with Gail's drunken face buried in her lap. Ricky pulled out and jacked off on the pair of them, Mo ignoring him as best she could.

Thirty seconds later Gail dissolved into tears. She dressed hurriedly, muttering apologies to Randy in heaven who watched the scene from atop a fluffy cloud strumming a harp. She entered her bedroom slamming the door as Maureen turned to Ricky, her face luminescent. She kissed Ricky full on the mouth.

"Stick with me, kid. We're gonna fuck until you can't stand it anymore!"

"Cool!" thought young Ricky.

Minutes later, Gail returned to the den with tears streaming from her face, turned up the sound on the television full blast and retreated to her bedroom again. Maureen dressed slowly, savoring the scent of Gail on her fingers. They left the house both fortified and resolute, Maureen already planning their next conquest. Together, the pair swung conspiratorially out of Gail's driveway, Mr. Leiber's Ford Pinto belching brown smoke at the sky.

{14}

A Mongoose in the Reptile House

†

LEX WAS STRUGGLING WITH A SQUARE of tinfoil, a box of baking soda and a lighter when Nina entered the attic where he had been hiding from the Dunderhearts. He'd picked up the coke smoking habit from the drummer in Mr. Big Stuff, a funk band he sometimes played keyboards for. Keeping on the down low had always seemed like the best course of action with that crew, but he was starting to see that pretty much anything went among the Dunderhearts as long as it didn't involve actually playing music. He had made up his mind just that morning to quit the habit, but the windfall of blow had made a mockery of his will power. Lex offered up the mirror with its small pile of mushy powder to Nina.

"I managed to kind of improvise some freebase with this tin foil and a pinch of baking soda…"

Nina removed four crack rocks the size of golf balls from her own bag, chipped off a piece of one and laid it in the bowl of a glass pipe.

"I had the Bolivians include some of these in the package to give it a little soul power."

She lit the rock taking a huge drag and holding it for as long as she could before beckoning Lex closer. She gently parted his lips and exhaled the second-hand smoke into his wanting lungs. For a moment their mouths touched, Nina's eyes remaining resolutely open. The dirty chemical smell of crack cocaine filled the room and they laughed, parties to a victimless crime that could easily destroy them. Lex took a hit and their lips met again, economy being the better part of drug abuse. Soon Nina was in his lap, carnal GPS set for his cock. Lex felt like the sharpest knife in a drawer that was nailed shut.

Nina's lips tasted like cherry life savers and butane and he kissed them until everything else disappeared. That familiar mind burning crack feeling ate at him from the inside and his mind started to race. Even with Nina's dramatic eye makeup on she looked to be about thirteen, but he knew that he was powerless to stop the coming explosion.

"How old are you, anyway?"

"I just turned eighteen," she might have lied.

Nina lit another rock and sat back. Inhaling penises was by now a basic part of her nature, but drugs were a very recent addition to the repertoire. She had never felt the need of artificial stimulants in the past, priding herself on an ability to master any situation and to prevail purely by force of her own indomitable will. She had maintained that attitude until meeting Ace at a house party and inhaling his particular penis. Ingesting him meant ingesting the drugs he'd ingested that night and her next several hours were spent grappling with, and then actually enjoying, the intoxication. As she began to spend more time with Ace she needed to eliminate half of her brain just to tolerate the conversations they had. She decided for the time being to imbibe what he imbibed and *love* was a word expressly prohibited from their vocabulary.

For Nina, the joy of assaulting her mind with all manner of compounds paled in comparison to the thrill of maintaining her composure while the rejects around her psychically crumbled. Keeping it together was the real buzz. If she hurt some feelings along the way or left a wicked scent across the corpse of some hipster's ego, well that was just a bonus. She would have to quit someday soon, she knew that, but for now drugs were just part of the woodwork. Her Lilliputian mouth engulfed Lex's Brobdingnagian cock like a mongoose in the reptile house.

{15}

Weighed and Found Wanting

†

FROM THE FLOOR OF MAGGORIO'S PUB, Ricky heard all things. He heard the excited buzz of humdrum lives interrupted by the best kind of violence, the kind that happens to someone else. He heard the undertone of impotent rage from Ronnie, the regret behind Bonnie's soothing consolations, the ineffectual huffing of Gretchen Maggorio, forced from behind the bar for the first time in months and brandishing an aluminum baseball bat. Ricky sensed subconsciously that he would survive, but his brain still needed to work out a few things before consciousness returned. What had he done to deserve the beating he'd gotten? He knew it had to be something dark and putrid, something that predated the placid homeowner he had so recently become.

"Baby...Please..."

Finally, the essence of Bonnie's pubis came to him through a kind of carnal synesthesia, a sort of pink meringue calypso monument. After a summer spent sampling vaginas in various stages of excitement, Bonnie's was like a little ray of springtime, delicate, savory, but still a long way from autumn's ripened waft. The combination of agile Maureen and docile Bonnie had been the pièce de résistance, the jewel in the crown of that perfect summer, the triple coupling that spoiled him for everything that had come after. He had known Bonnie a thousand times since then in his dreams, her face losing shape and contour, her hairstyle a distant memory. That exquisitely mixed bag that was her vagina, though, became a template by which all others would forever be weighed in the balance and found wanting. He had stuck his face in it gladly, wearing the glorious residue like a badge of honor. Back in the numinous fog of history, perhaps Ponce de Leon had searched in vain for the fountain of youth that nestled between the shapely thighs of Bonnie Naylor, now Marquette.

And therein lay the rub. Ronnie had marked Bonnie's territory sophomore year and never once had he wavered in his commitment to her since then. Bonnie, too, had maintained a near perfect record of fidelity, except for that one summer transgression, weepingly confessed in a spasm of honesty the night before they were wed. This carnal knowledge had poked at Ronnie like a burr beneath his saddle for twenty-eight long years.

Though the floor of Maggorio's was sticky with gum and ash and spit that mocked Ricky like a shoe in the mouth, still that enchanting pussy ran forth with fresh spring water. That summer like no other was all he'd ever wanted, simply to fuck and fuck again and have all the ensuing psychic debts paid off by osmosis. Even now, he preferred this dirty barroom floor to the certain knowledge that the best time of his life had happened so quickly and such a long, long time ago. Dead to the world, he smiled while Ronnie raged on and Bonnie's honeyed tones finally melted the glacier of his anger. At long last, together, they strolled through the swinging doors of Maggorio's and out into the parking lot, heads held high to face the small predictable world beyond. From his roost on the floor, Ricky smiled on.

In his mind's eye his cock was embedded in Bonnie's pussy, her face buried in Maureen's substantial 1980s muff. He fucked her and stared over her back at Mo's green eyes fixed on the ceiling, her hands firmly gripping Bonnie's hair as she grinded across that forgettable face and climaxed with a gratuitous shimmy before licking her juices off Bonnie's vanquished lips.

Decades after the fact, Ricky had paid the price for defiling another man's reason for living. Now, Ricky needed a reason, too. Never much for introspection while conscious, unconsciously he craved a life larger than his own. Despite legends to the contrary, humans use quite a bit more than ten percent of their brains. That doesn't make us smart, though. In the parts of his brain that he wasn't using, Ricky resolved to be like a ray of light dancing across the heavens, his only purpose to spread joy and expand consciousness. No longer tethered by earthly desires, secure in the knowledge that he was master of a destiny inextricably linked to that of mankind itself and to every imaginable vista great and microbial, he prepared his soul to return to the land of the living. Come what may, he would rise up off of this stinking floor and be whole for the first time since that endless summer had ended. He would make the old ice cream truck that was his heart shiny and new for all of the damaged children everywhere; rejuvenated, recharged, Ricky Lee would soar again!

Alas, when consciousness did return it still inhabited the unremarkable form of Richard Elliot Leiber, unchanged and unchangeable.

{16}

Eating It, Too

✝

NINA CONCENTRATED ON A BALL OF GREY DUST that gently rippled in the corner and felt Lex's cock move rhythmically in and then out as her third orgasm loomed. Like a couple in therapy, he did all the work. Lex, his muscular form bathed in sweat, pounded like a man possessed. In the past he'd found it difficult to perform on drugs, now he found it impossible to stop. It might have been the excitement of a possible beating from Ace, the proximity of dead bodies nearby or maybe just the drugs, but he suspected the real cause was Nina West herself. She was simply born to fuck, endowed by her creator with all of the attributes that inspired the sacking of ancient Troy.

The taste, feel, sight and smell of her intoxicated him as no other had and as he sawed away at this animated porcelain doll he finally realized how he could have tolerated this stint with the talentless Dunderhearts: he coveted the band's only spectator. Now he was having his cake and eating it, too. Brain on fire from the drugs, he knew that he loved her, there was no use denying it. He'd follow her to the ends of the Earth or just to the supermarket to buy tampons. Nina grew bored. She enjoyed fucking Lex, but she'd come thrice now and he showed no signs of letting up or letting go. Even the skills acquired through constant repetition of her Kegels, the only exercise regimen she could commit to, had failed to bring forth a load from the burly bassist. She decided to unleash the big guns.

"Fuck me baby...fill my pussy..."

Nina generally figured the less said the better. No matter how good a slice of pizza was she never addressed it on the plate or begged it to do tricks for her. Why humans needed constant reassurance that their genitals were functioning correctly was beyond her understanding, but verbalizing had done the trick with these all-night types before when all else had failed. Her voice was somewhat *contralto* for such a petite creature, but she pitched it up at times like this, aware that squealing connoted innocence and submission that in turn suggested victory for the male ego.

"...come all over my slutty little ass...spank it..."

Lex felt almost sober as he entered the astral plane, hovering over his own frantically undulating body. While he could clearly see himself, he was much more interested in Nina's gently curved gluteus that bucked and writhed under the weight of him. He felt like Apollo 13 gliding through the vast reaches of an infinite space so tight it threatened to cut his prick off. He was Magellan and Cortes, Hefner and Lovelace, Abbott and Costello. She was all that he could see, hear or experience, her genitals the Alpha and Omega of blissful congress.

He raised his right hand triumphantly over his head and felt a searing pain well up in his chest like hot knives through the aorta. Three seconds later he was dead.

{17}

Black
Fireworks

†

THEY SAY THAT PARIS IS A WHORE. If that's true than Highland Falls is a hand job from a crippled transvestite behind a 7-Eleven. Economically advantaged, culturally barren and infuriatingly bourgeois it fell into a fitful restless sleep around ten pm and awoke with a fart and a cough promptly at six. Ricky Lee limped its empty streets contemplating closing time. He had vetoed the proffered ambulance, emergency room and police station, leaving Maggorio's under his own steam and reasoning that the walk would clear his head. As he left the strip malls of Mount Highland behind and entered the manicured subdivisions of Highland Oaks and finally Highland Falls itself his mood was dismal.

Ricky hadn't been chin checked since the sixth grade and every part of him ached, but none worse than his ego. He'd almost forgotten he had one, but now it came roaring back in crimson dreams of revenge. He wanted to tie that ignorant townie to a tree and flog the fucking jackass, still fighting for the long lost honor of his dullard sweetheart. What cut deepest was the realization that Ricky had never cared for anyone enough to throw a punch, not even for himself. Allison was someone to fight with, not for. Still he wondered where she was, who she was with and why he had walked out of one empty house and into another.

"Excuse me, sir, can we see some identification?"

The police car pulled up next to Ricky like an old neighbor who's fallen and can't get up. An aggressive incompetence emanated from the driver, a prim sullenness from his partner on the passenger side who did the talking. Ricky viewed all police as a threat, but somehow these two appeared more lost and unsure than himself. He reached in his pocket only to realize he'd lost his wallet and ID in the scuffle and still had half of the joint he'd shared with Feet hours before. He was beaten and bruised, ashamed and alone and he had no faith in Highland justice. Thoughts began to ricochet through his head overloading his brain and he panicked and ran.

He ran down streets lined with cute little shops and shaded tables where ladies ate lunch. He ran past meticulously planned outdoor oases lined with parking spaces for mighty vehicles that transported the well-to-do hither and yon. He ran past the four hundred and forty yards of track that circled the back of Highland High and he ran still more, lungs burning, feet swollen and bent. He ran until he could no longer think of Doris and Morris and Allison and That Dyke Maureen and That Magic Cunt Bonnie and That Nymph from the Funeral Home...

Ricky wiped the sweat from his eyes to remove the mirage, but the image persisted. That same girl from the funeral service was exiting Minarini's through the side door in the middle of the night. She looked fragile holding a flashlight in the darkness, her face casting an eerie glow as three young men struggled under the weight of a massive white bag. They reached the hearse and loaded it, then gunned the motor and headed off into the night. Nina became that part of the darkness that swallows the light, desire itself erupting like black fireworks in the sky. She shined her light in a semicircle around the property feeling unseen eyes upon her.

"Hey, I met you the other day..."

The frown that had already begun its inevitable creep across her features told a story he had heard too many times before. The tongue was dry and rubbery in his mouth, knees buckling, palms oozing with sweat. Resigned to a final kamikaze effort he attempted the unbearable and just told the truth.

"The cops are after me, I'm running away. Please...can you... hide me?"

She said nothing. She did nothing. She felt nothing. He took her inscrutable expression for an affirmative, worming past her through the open door. He wasn't home, but he was right where he wanted to be. Nina bolted the door behind them.

{18}

Li'l Orphan Nina

✝

"WHY DON'T WE JUST DUMP HIM by the hospital and take off?" suggested Easy. "It's not like we killed the guy."

Ace envied Easy his limited comprehension of death investigations. After two years on the job hauling carcasses from accident sites he knew them only too well. Life may indeed be cheap, but the overtime paid to a nosy cop, lab technician or private eye on the trail of a homicide suspect was not. At the very least there would be hours of questioning and paperwork; there would have to be statements from each individual involved and a complete search of the funeral home and the stickiest questions of all would concern Nina.

For openers, how did a teenage orphan with a bloodstream full of drugs come to be caught *in flagrante delicto* with a dead body inside a mortuary in the middle of the night? When the band had walked in on the two of them, Nina was applying a curious form of oral resuscitation to Lex. Though he was clearly dead it appeared that rigor mortis had only affected one part of his anatomy, and that part was so large Nina had resembled a baby boa imbibing a marmoset. The cops would want to know everything that Ace didn't want to remember.

Unfortunately, kicking the shit out of Lex just wasn't an option anymore. As the hearse rolled on the band argued about what radio station to tune in, forgetting that across America's airwaves all roads lead to nowhere. Ace didn't know much, but he knew that the most complete method of disposal would be to feed Lex to a herd of hungry swine. When they got through with him every trace would be gone. Downstate, near Carbondale, two old hippies named Nestor and Willow ran a ranch that practiced holistic animal husbandry, grew soybeans and trimmed cheap weed grown by local farmers. They also threw unauthorized parties, dubbed 'Throwbacks', to introduce new club drugs they had synthesized. The full kilo of Nina's uncut coke he had brought to barter would make their sudden appearance plausible enough and once he could sneak out to the pigpens and dispose of the body they'd be home free.

"Goddamn Lex," thought Ace.

By the time the Dunderhearts pulled up to the Bar Out Ranch the coke had mostly worn off, Birdie falling into fitful chunks of sleep apnea in the back seat. Ace had kept his eyes on the road, his hands upon the wheel all four and a half hours from Highland Falls to the boondocks as gray fingers of sunlight began to creep over the horizon. Their fearless leader may have been dumb, but he wasn't lacking in self-preservation instincts. He knew he should have just turned the body over to the sheriff's office, but the thought of losing Nina made anything he might gain playing it safe seem trivial. Now, he had taken the band on a midnight run as if they were all in this together, when truly he was the only one with anything to lose.

"Where are we and why are we?"

Birdie felt sick to his stomach as he awoke in a big black car stinking of feet and ass in the middle of nowhere. His friends were dropping like flies and he half wished to be next and all he really wanted was a drink to take the edge off. Conversely, Easy had fallen asleep as soon as the hearse had started rolling and woke refreshed and ready to take on a brand new day. He grabbed for the bottle of White Claw at his feet, took a long swig and barked-

"Where's that fucking coke!"

Ace instinctively back handed him across the bridge of his nose without turning around, an astounding feat of dexterity, if not fairness. Here he grew serious and turned around, locking eyes with Birdie and Easy to bring the drama home.

"Just stay cool until we know what's what here, keep to the mission and follow me. Whatever you do, don't draw any attention to yourselves. Tonight, the Dunderhearts lost one of our own; today we bury him so nobody ever finds out. More than anything we've gone through, gentlemen, this act binds us together. For the very first time we truly are a band!"

It was a rousing speech, the kind Ace wasn't really sincere enough to deliver, but a lifetime of late night television and years of listening to funeral oration had made him a toastmaster by proxy. He didn't believe a word of it. Lex was the only one in the band who ever had a shot at anything and he was about to be pig food. Ace just hoped these two dipshits could keep their mouths shut and their noses clean long enough to let him get the job done. He laid out three big rails scraped from the brick he'd brought. Stashing it under the seat, he immediately snorted a line and offered some to Birdie before Easy could pull any tricks. This maneuver allowed Easy to reach under the seat and steal the entire bag, but Ace's ability to see the forest had always been marred by the uncanny existence of trees.

{19}

Pearls Before Tinkerbell

†

RICKY WANTED NINA AS HE HAD never wanted anything in his life and it scared him. He wanted her to hold his hand and cook him breakfast and tell him everything was going to be OK. He wanted her to worry when he came home late and iron his favorite shirt and pull his rod out during a romantic comedy starring Katherine Heigl and Paul Rudd. He wanted to die and be reborn as whatever she wanted him to be. He wanted, more than anything, for her to want him, knowing deep in his marrow that she did not.

"It's been a trying night…um?"

"…Ricky."

"Ricky, it's been a frustrating evening in a variety of ways. I won't bore you with the details, but why don't you strip naked and eat my pussy?"

Why not indeed? Ricky was sure he had just had an aural hallucination, but a lifetime of scrounging and lounging had taught him never to pass up a free meal. He rose to his feet and removed his shirt, thankful that poverty had kept him trim if less than toned. Though his eye had begun to swell shut and it ached each time he drew breath, he felt elated inside.

Nina removed her shirt revealing breasts so pert they might have been hors d'oeuvres at a tea party thrown by Tinkerbell. She looked at Ricky not with lust, but sympathy. True, she had killed a man with narcotics and sex earlier in the evening, but clearly this guy was hurting. Nina's vagina nestled in soft turquoise panties like a down shorn peach. To cover it in pubic hair would be like tattooing the Mona Lisa or adding a Jay-Z intro to Bach's Fugue in D Minor. True, Ricky had once conquered Bonnie Naylor's Mount McKinley, but the Everest that surely lay between the thighs of Nina West seemed impossibly high with air so thin one would die like fish on a carpet mounting its narrow vastness.

Ricky subscribed to the theory that in the presence of food the fool goes hungry. He habitually took what was offered to him, be it a cigar, a half-eaten burrito or a life changing sexual experience. Nina had always been comfortable casting the pearls of her sexuality before the swine that comprised the human race. It was her particular cross to bear as she imagined a tiara of thorns causing little rhythmic arcs of red to pulsate gently down her pale face, the sun setting over Golgotha. Ricky kissed her and achieved what Buddhists call bodhicitta. Inside of that magic embrace, to simply serve her was his fondest wish. He realized in a flash of clarity that Nina was a perfected being, that when they united his heart would somehow purify and his life would be made complete.

Nina hadn't had a death free orgasm in several hours. Lex's demise had sullied the evening and she viewed the appearance of this unremarkable zero as faint reward. In her morbid fantasies she would pretend that Ricky *was* the late Lex, perfect physique, enormous boner and all. To be fucked by a dead man was a kick even she hadn't considered before. With this sad sack as surrogate she planned to get her nightly ration, all while dutiful Ace buried the evidence downstate. In that moment, she even sort of loved them all, every brainless agglomeration of XY chromosomes that trudged the earth. Then Ricky was inside of her. What he lacked in girth and hygiene she compensated for in imagination. Lex had been all those things a girl wants a boy to be: gorgeous and dead, and though she preferred another penis to the one currently invading her, that was a woman's prerogative. For the next thirty minutes, fueled by hormones, adrenaline, shame, powdered reuptake inhibitors and just a whiff of lavender body oil, Ricky Lee made love like a man reborn.

{20}

The Maroon
Curtain

†

NOSES FROZEN AND BRAINS AFOG, Birdie, Easy and Ace
followed their ears into an enormous aluminum silo. Trance music
boomed from speakers haphazardly dotting the walls and ceiling
that accentuated a deafening phase incoherence. The entire structure shook both with the loudness of the bass and the aftershock
of a dozen sources of sound hitting a hundred dirty eardrums at
almost the same time. Lights flickered and dimmed and strobed and
refracted in mute deference to the cacophony, illuminating in bursts
the bodies dancing or convulsing on the makeshift dance floor.

"Looks like last night's party is petering out. I'm going to see if I can
find Willow and Nestor by the barn out back. Just try to blend in for
a bit."

Birdie didn't know what blending in here might mean. If it meant
donning frumpy unisex overalls or chewing on faux neon lightsticks
he wanted no part of it. Birdie hated hippies, which he defined as
anyone with a bad hairstyle who needed a bath, did drugs and didn't
feel guilty about it afterward.

"What brings you two square pegs to this round hole so early in the
AM?"

The question was posed by a stocky garden gnome of a man
dressed in purple brocade with gold piping and a velvet hat with
a blue dahlia pinned to the side that might have embarrassed a

seventeenth century French courtier. Though pleased that someone here had gone to the trouble of dressing up, Birdie vacillated between a wish to ignore him completely or shit in his hat. The stranger's limpid hazel eyes locked on Easy with a sniper's intensity, searching that vacant face for signs of intelligence. Finding none he pressed on.

"You two aren't from around here, are you? I'm thinking Palatine or Arlington Heights…maybe Kankakee?"

He extended a plump hand toward Easy.

"Did you hear about the Throwback on social media? I'm always floored by the quality DJ's they lure out here, I guess it just requires the right…inducements."

His voice rose excruciatingly on that last word. Birdie looked around at the dregs of the party, hipsters with eyes like saucers mixing with country bumpkins determined to sleep with someone more attractive than their second cousin. Lost, wired and upset Birdie just wanted this evening to end and he wanted a martini, dry, fuck the olive. Gideon, sensing his quarry's love of substance abuse, pulled out a glossy fold and opened it, offering it to Easy who blurted triumphantly, "*Coke!*" wasting no time in snorting the entire pile.

"Not exactly…"

Easy's nose was now on fire and within seconds he fell to his knees, blood pouring like the Hoover Dam. His mind, disoriented at the best of times, began to resemble a painting by Jackson Pollack stuffed with nitroglycerin, sprinkled with napalm and set ablaze in a blast furnace.

"Me grandma dice…klezmer recombinant horseshoe…Kanpai!"

Easy collapsed to the floor in a flurry of nonsensical verbiage, his brain short circuiting just before the maroon curtain fell on his consciousness. Birdie knelt over him, feeling for a pulse and checking his ragged breathing. Gideon said only-

"Oh my, that is a shame. Fortunately, I am a doctor of sorts."

{21}

A Reptilian State

✝

RICKY LEE HAD FALLEN IN LOVE WITH NINA at first sight. Now that he had actually lain with her, words like *cherish* or even *worship* couldn't contain his swollen feelings. He simply knew that come what may he must be by her side doing whatever pleased her until he dropped dead and she found a suitable use for his remains. Then he would go on serving her until Time and Space collided eons hence.

For her part, Nina wanted a pizza, pepperoni and olive, dusted liberally with parmesan and she wanted a Coca-Cola. What she didn't want was Ricky Lee, or Richard Leiber for that matter, both of whom could fall off the edge of the Earth, preferably now. He had made her come though, so when he drifted off to sleep she stifled the urge to wake him up just to throw him out. There were no services scheduled for tomorrow and Ricky looked so peaceful sleeping, a simpering grin on his pedestrian face, that she let him be.

Nina left the room quietly, descending stairs still slick from Lex's expirations and hurtled ass over tea kettle toward the floor waiting far below. The rush of tumbling through the void exhilarated her and the first non-ironic smile in a decade spread across her face. Stomach light with expectation, mind roaming free, she straddled dimensions of sight and sound and light and color. Nina pulsated like an amoeba ready to burst and multiply, she soared like a butterfly freed from a silken cocoon. For an instant, she felt the sensation of absolute freedom, a limitless place where all things are possible. Saint Peter, Rhiannon and Vishnu stopped by to chat, but Nina shined them on just to be bratty.

Then she hit the floor at the bottom of that long flight of stairs with a bang that woke Ricky from his slumber. He rose quickly, not bothering to put his clothes on as he hurried across the room. From the top of the stairs he saw Nina's limp form oozing darkness below. He slid down the banister like a fireman descending his pole, reaching her in seconds. An overwhelming sense of loss and dread flooded over him, the deaths of Morris and Doris suddenly pale in comparison. Gently he turned her over, relieved to find her unconscious, but breathing. Mercifully, the source of the blood seemed to be her nose and he lifted her up, cradling her in his arms tenderly. Ricky wasn't strong, but she was light. He gazed into her closed eyelids and saw the shadow of an angel. He liked her this way, beautiful and helpless, belonging to him alone. Eventually, she would awaken and replace him with somebody better, but in this glorious moment Ricky Lee had everything he'd ever wanted.

He strolled around the funeral parlor slowly, the object of his affection nestled in his arms; into the chapel with its high ceiling and carefully non-sectarian imagery, the viewing room with its somber curtains and subdued lighting and finally to the little nook where he had slept during his parents' service, the first place Nina had spoken to him. It was in this building, the Highland Falls Funeral Home, family owned and operated since nineteen-forty-something that they had met and then consummated their love and so he loved this sacred place, every word that had ever been spoken here, every imperfect being that had spent its last moments above ground here. In that instant, he loved everything and everyone, but especially Nina West. Ricky glowed with an inner light that exhilarated him. He was back where he belonged. He would thrive, survive and even triumph against all odds and one day she would truly be his, right here in Highland Falls.

He turned around then, her limp body still breathing softly against his chest, to find old Fredo Minarini facing him cane held high. Ricky was naked, his cock dangling beneath the still unconscious Nina. Fredo was old, but this was his territory and he brought the cane down hard across Ricky's forehead. Ricky's first instinct was to give up, but as he sank to his knees he realized the precious cargo his arms contained. He held onto her resolutely as Fredo rained blow after blow upon his face and skull. He had gone in one evening from humiliation to satisfaction to horror to elation and now to simple pain so quickly that his mind reverted to a gelatinous state.

He carefully placed Nina on the floor, passing his hand over her mouth to make sure she was still respiratory. Smelling the Vick's Vape-O-Rub on Minarini's chest, blinded by blood, sweat and fear, he found his footing and somehow found the big oak door, finally finding himself outside and naked in the unforgiving daylight. He ran one long block to the home of his youth, faster than he had ever run before, graying testicles flapping toward his unshod feet.

{ 22 }

The Ninalithic Era

✝

NINA EMERGED NAKED, HER HAIR in pigtails amid a field of black daisies. A giant centaur galloped by and she grabbed for his erection like the saddle horn of a pony. He deposited her on the side of a vast cliff face where she looked out upon a bright red ocean that glistened under a hot pink sun. Ships sailed and docked in the harbor and strong tanned pirates with long dark hair and snaggle teeth moved about their decks purposefully. The smell of tanning butter and rum wafted over the horizon and Nina began to dance like a go-go girl in a 1960's discotheque. She did the Frug, the Watusi, the Twist, the Stomp and the Mashed Potato, too. Superior to you, me and everyone else, Nina had attained in less than two decades what Gautama Buddha had spent a lifetime striving and then not striving and then striving again to attain. And she did it with a much flatter stomach, her bunny-like feces odorless and her vagina running forth with fresh pear nectar. Awakening in this realm where wishes came true, embodying the Universal Will was all in a day's play. In dreams, the only reality that could contain her, Nina thrived untethered, soared free like the wind and took from the Earth just what she wanted, seeing and understanding all like God Almighty. For Nina West it wasn't enough to be fearless, not anymore; and bewildering as it might be for us to comprehend in our own timid epoch, enlightened scholars of the future will someday call this moment the dawning of the Ninalithic Era.

And then it was over.

She opened her eyes to the site of Fredo Minarini, baggy pants around his ankles, wizened penis in one hand working his ancient prostate with the fingers of the other. Faded brown socks showed against pale lumpy shins, his gut arched over his genitals as if to shield them from shame. Flecks of spittle gathered around the edges of his chapped and arid mouth.

As he saw Nina's eyes flutter open his chest palpitated and he orgasmed, a dry but heartfelt burst from deep within. One wan teardrop of semen fell to the floor by his feet. He raised a hand as if composing something important to say, then sagged to the ground heavily, breathing his last. Nina crawled toward where he lay and licked the floor clean as a final teasing memorial to her employer. As the lights dimmed behind his rheumy eyes she realized that this man was like every other man, no better or worse, no smarter or kinder. But, he was gone now and might prove useful.

{23}

Twinkle
Falling
Stars

✝

ACE HAD FAILED TO FIND WILLOW OR NESTOR or anyone else he knew. A sort of pregnant calm prevailed all over the farm except for the far away din of revelers at the silo. He scanned the horizon, dreading his imminent come down, that age-old dilemma of crash now or keep snorting. He resolved to do the latter after disposing of Lex. Hearing the sound of pigs at play, a sound at once joyful and industrious, he hurried back to the hearse anxious to consume more cocaine. First, he opened the back and untied the white sack that contained his fallen comrade. He had to admit it, Lex was a good-looking guy. Even in death he had somehow maintained his sense of style. Ace closed the bag, slammed the door and drove across the muddy pasture to where a dozen spotted pigs frolicked in shards of grey morning light.

He looked around at the manicured vastness and wondered why anybody would work on a farm doing chores. Why not escape to the mountains, the woods, the ocean, anywhere but here? He'd rather be a drummer than live like that. He reached under the driver's seat for the kilo and found it gone. Panic gripped his scrotum, then his heart and finally his mind. Confusion, realization and then anger followed and he fantasized about beating Easy to a pulp and feeding what remained of him to the hogs. He'd deal with that little kook later. Furiously, he stormed to the back of the body wagon, lifted the corpse out of the bag and trudged toward the pigpen. When he got there, he heaved Lex into the enclosure and heard-

"Damn!"

The voice stopped Ace dead in his tracks. Was it possible that he had just fed a living man to a pack of ravenous swine? That would be a horrible thing, of course, but if Lex had actually managed to fuck Nina then surely it represented a just punishment. As long as Ace had her he wouldn't share her, not with anybody. Jealousy clawed at his insides as he caught the glimmer of a spider's web in an empty barn doorframe. Unfortunately, nothing clever or profound was spelled out inside the web about the assembled pigs that continued to snort and tussle in the chill of gathering daybreak.

"What's shaking?"

The woman asking the question seemed to pop up out of the muck dressed in torn overalls, her dilated eyes streaked with mascara and glitter that twinkled like falling stars. It was hard to tell if she was a farm hand, a local or a visitor from another dimension entirely. She held up Lex's right arm and asked-

"This guy a friend of yours?"

The pigs began to amble curiously toward the body laying ghastly white while the sun gained strength on the horizon. A crooked smile played over the woman's face as she extended a filthy hand toward Ace. When he clasped it, she pulled him to her deep in the dirt of the pigpen. She laughed then, nuzzling into his shoulder exclaiming-

"Molly!?"

That was either her name or a question he didn't have the answer to. He noticed that she was cute in a rotten sort of way and very strong. Ace instantly felt that he had known her for a long time, but wasn't sure if she was friend or foe, an accomplice or an accident waiting to happen, a succubus sent to destroy him or just the dirty girl next door. He hoped she was all this and more.

"You're high as fuck, aren't you!" Molly exclaimed, her voice suddenly ringing with desire. Ace knew that loose drug talk mixed with the cadaver could wind up badly for him in court, but what kind of a narc hung out among herds of swine at six in the morning?

"I had some coke…"

"I looove coke, fucking love it," she said, lashes blinking as she reverentially contemplated the glory of C17H21NO4. She looked Ace full in the face, her eyes a well of dilated sincerity.

"I really need some, otherwise I might stop drinking," she smiled again, playfully nudging Lex's prone form where it lay in the mud. The hogs grunted and kicked up clods of earth around them. For Ace the moment froze, as he contemplated Molly like a warped vision of Our Lady complete with natural backdrop, soft focus and barnyard aromas.

She leaned over Lex then and unhooked his big silver belt buckle. Removing his pants in one deft swipe she took his cock in her mouth, eyes glued on Ace the entire time. She fussed on Lex's dead organ brazenly as if auditioning for a no-budget film and soon, contrary to the laws of biology, the expired penis came to life in her mouth. Witnessing a miracle, Ace felt preternaturally aware, his ears open to the snuffling of pigs, the guttural sounds of Molly's debauchery, the faraway thump of electronic music and the ultraviolet sound of blue sky emerging full blown from the dreary gray that had imprisoned the morning.

Molly coaxed the doomed bassist's post mortem erection and then rode it proudly, beating time with her frowzy knit cap as she slipped and slid in the moist sludge of the pen. In due time, she came loudly like a circus elephant at a Tuvan throat opera, extracting the very last fluid ounce of Lexington Concord Rumsfeld III. When she turned around for the reverse mount, Ace could contain himself no longer. Feelings began to stir in the cavity where his heart was alleged to be. He'd always known he was capable of anything that required neither brains nor talent; finally, he had found a creature who could match him note for sour note. He grabbed her roughly and took by force what she offered freely, after first making a great show of flinging his rival Lex's remains to the exuberantly squealing hogs.

While the pigs masticated Lex, Ace and Molly made the beast with two backs. They burrowed into one another like moles, sweating and slobbering and eventually climaxing together in the dirt.

When it was over, they embraced almost tenderly, her slightly mis-shapen head resting on his poorly tattooed chest. Two pigs fought over some last morsels from the feast, loudly grappling and kicking up grime until a nine-inch chunk of meat sailed through the Midwestern ether making a ponderous arc over the oppressive air of the pigpen.

Two point four seconds later, Lex's enormous penis landed squarely on the upturned faces of Molly and Ace simultaneously, its massive girth casting a shadow over the newly minted pair that lay like a vow unspoken. Now, they were one.

"That dead dude was pretty fucking hot!" said Molly as roosters crowed a brand new day.

{24}

Downright Nauseating

†

EASY BREATHED RESTFULLY, EYES CLOSED mouth open, a beatific smile on his face. For his part, Birdie could already feel the beating Ace would give them both when he found out the Dunder-hearts had failed to blend in with the crowd.

"What the hell is wrong, what did you give him?"

"It's harmless, just an amalgam of various animal tranquilizers. He must have a delicate constitution."

Birdie wanted to run somewhere far away. He knew Ace would be furious because Ace was always furious about nothing and this was actually something. Between the kilo of booger sugar and Lex's corpse lay a landmine of felonies. The weekend he had spent in Highland County lockup for a gram of hash and two failures to appear had seemed severe at the time, but now he saw the maximum security specter of Joliet looming before him. Curious ravers peered across the room at Easy prone on the floor.

"Somebody better do something fast!"

Gideon clapped his hands and two enormous Haitians material-ized in matching white Capri pants with white suspenders crisscross-ing their bare chests. They were both so massive it appeared that Huey and Louie had eaten Dewey and returned for seconds.

"Take him to the chopper, *tout de suite!*"

Birdie followed helplessly as Easy was carried through the crowd and out to a rundown heliport perched where cattle once grazed. A pilot and stewardess in matching vintage aviation outfits scurried into the idling helicopter gleaming in the early morning sun. Fearing he might be losing his mind Birdie posed a simple question-

"Who the fuck *are* you, Mister?"

"Dr. Gideon Balzfyre. I make records."

The little purple man doffed his outrageous hat and bowed low, but then couldn't get up again. He motioned to one of his attendants to right him while the other pulled two muscle relaxers out of a plastic bag and shoved them into his mouth. The little man swallowed them dry.

"You mean like...Balzfyre Records?"

"The very same."

Unless you never watched television, listened to the radio or surfed the interweb, Dr. Giddy needed no introduction. He had written and produced dozens of Top 40, country and R&B hits; he'd been a force on the airwaves and in the executive suites of Hollywood, New York, and Nashville for longer than most pop stars had been alive; and in the realms of television and multimedia he'd helped to create scores of young pop idols since the premier of his talent showcase *American Showstopper*. Dr. Gideon Balzfyre held a doctorate in music theory from Indiana University. A scandal involving members of a high school glee club, a tub of Crisco and a hustler named JonJon had derailed his first career as a music teacher, but academia's loss had turned out to be the music industry's gain. For two decades now, he had racked up hit after hit by giving the people what they wanted: new versions of things they'd already heard. He brushed off the plagiarism lawsuits as jealousy, the cost of doing business; hailed as a reclusive genius, he reasoned that one out of two ain't bad.

In short, Dr. Giddy reigned over the entertainment industry like a bona fide renaissance hack and somehow, in mid-nowhere Illinois, fate and a beautiful corpse had put Brian 'Birdie' Kornfelter next to a legend. For the first time in his life he found a reason for optimism.

As the Haitians loaded Easy onto the chopper and began minister-ing to him, Birdie ran back on to the dance floor, scrawled a note on the back of a rave flyer and handed it to the first person he saw, telling her to give it to an angry looking guy named Ace. By the time he returned, the pilot had given Balzfyre the thumbs up for takeoff and he motioned for Birdie to climb aboard.

"Let's head toward my ranch in Nashville and see what shakes out. When your friend comes around we can hole up for a while and get better acquainted. I do so hope we can all be…friends."

He looked deeply into Birdie's eyes, exuding the kind of trustwor-thiness and concern that only those who can't be trusted and don't really care can. Balzfyre turned and gazed wistfully at Easy lying on the stretcher, his breathing deep and steady, his wiry frame com-pact and muscular, his expression catatonic. Dr. Giddy snapped his fingers and one of the enormous islanders unzipped Easy's fly and pulled his dirty Levi's down. The producer took Easy's cock in his mouth and began kissing it like a child with its first kitten.

"You don't think he'd mind, do you Mr. Birdie?"

Birdie contemplated Easy prone on the floor of the chopper, a noncommittal expression on his face, his valiant little Johnson at half-mast and rising. Birdie knew that nonconsensual sex was wrong in all cases and that homosexuality, at least the male version, could be downright nauseating. This was surely a betrayal of his band-mate and a violation of basic human decency, but Easy had done all the man's drugs…maybe he had it coming?

"André, come over here and lick these little balls won't you? Hervé, put your asshole on his nose and wiggle around some, hmmm?"

Birdie fantasized about a lucrative career in entertainment while Easy dreamed of a goat he had fed at a Milwaukee petting zoo one summer long ago.

{25}

Only the Ice Cream Truck

†

RICKY AWOKE TO THE SOUND OF HIS PARENTS' bed moving under the combined muscle power of three young men from Taiwan. For a moment, he thought he might be dead and attempted to fall back asleep, but the aches and bruises of last night throbbed him wide awake. Feeling like a Roman emperor in his decline he allowed himself to be carried outside and deposited on the front lawn. Clad only in well worn boxer shorts he dismounted the bed unnoticed by the chattering workmen.

A yellow box truck yawned open stuffed to the brim with the contents of his childhood home. There was the Nordic Trak exercise bike (still in mint condition) and the barbecue grill (in decidedly worse condition); the pots and pans, old books and older records; the bath mats, linen rollers and glue gun, all the detritus of Morris' and Doris' domestic existence and all of it stacked precariously as though destined for the junk heap. An elderly man directed the operation wielding a megaphone and barking in Mandarin. He approached Ricky and gave him a smack on the side of the head.

"No garage sale today! You trespassing now!"

"That's my stuff, I live here!"

Panic seized Ricky and he ran back into the house. All the trappings of suburban life were vanishing around him leaving only antiquated wallpaper and emptiness. The same bleak spectacle greeted him in the bedrooms, the den, the kitchen and rec room. He ran to the garage where the sporty Lexus and reliable minivan had also vanished. Only the incongruous ice cream truck remained. On the kitchen counter a pile of unopened mail sat gathering dust. Ricky felt cold in the pit of his gut. He randomly selected a letter and opened it.

> This is your final notice, failure to remit the balance in full will result in repossession and forfeiture of the vehicle and could lead to civil penalties...

In addition to the car repos there were notices from Aaronson's Furniture and Best Buy Electronics, from Sprint, Macy's and HBO and the Midwest Mortgage and Title Company. There was even one from the Highland Falls Funeral Home.

Five days would now encompass the sum total of Ricky's permanent retirement. Five days for the future to dissolve before his eyes. The dream was dead, a sham from start to finish. This was the hill he would die on wounded and beaten and it just wasn't fair. Hot tears fell down his face, a lump grew in his throat. He really was a loser, losing again, like the lottery player who tells his boss to shove it up his ass before realizing he's off by just one number. Well, this time he wouldn't stand for the fuzzy end of the lollipop!

He walked to the garage and grabbed for a metal rake that stood against the wall, brandishing it like a baseball bat. Teeth gritted, he strode out to the lawn and swung, connecting with the heads of Yang Wei and Jimmy Liu before they knew they were even under attack. Yang, a recent graduate of Highland Junior College and Liu, a martial arts enthusiast of limited skill, wobbled briefly on their heels before piling into the truck; the third mover dropped the object he was carrying and ran so fast down the block he forgot his own name making it unnecessary to transcribe it here. The old man with the megaphone clambered into the driver's seat locking the doors and gunning the engine, the whole event over just forty seconds after it had begun.

Ricky was not a violent man by nature, but discomfort and the prospect of returning to the ranks of the employed had driven him temporarily insane.

{26}

A Feral
Beast

†

ACE AND MOLLY RETURNED TO THE RAVE hand in hand, Lex's cock dangling on a shoelace around her neck like a child's macaroni necklace. His mission accomplished, Ace craved cocaine, though the band had disappeared with it and were no doubt halfway through the brick by now. While this might have aroused his rage just an hour ago, recent events had altered his perspective. Since his tryst with Molly, an emotionally driven and discontented Ace had given way to a more pragmatic one. If the coke was gone, perhaps they could score some ketamine at the rave; if the band was gone, so be it, he didn't really like rock music anyway; and though the pair of them stank like pigs in shit, these hippies wouldn't notice in the general funk of the place.

Then he remembered Nina. Though she'd replace him in a heartbeat, to give her up for any reason at all seemed like madness. He began to feel sick to his stomach, as if the elevator of his future had plummeted from the top of what used to be the Sears Tower. He took a deep breath, closed his eyes and took stock of the situation. Molly had already attached herself to him and was sure to be an unending source of calamity until they wound up dead in a ditch somewhere. Still, there seemed a predictability to her chaos. If given the chance she'd always go wrong one hundred percent of the time. Nina, by contrast, had a maddening tendency to zig after zagging, throwing him off his game and making him feel small and inferior, even with his cum dripping off her face.

Ace knew that Nina was a cut above anything he deserved, but he was sick of eating steak and craved a slider, sure that he'd starve soon anyway.

"Excuse me, are you Ace? Your friends left this note for you."

Scrawled on the back of a rave flyer were the words-

WE QUIT

The Dunderhearts were the only thing Ace had ever created and he loved them like he loved himself, that is to say not very much. Despite this betrayal he felt a sensation of freedom. From this moment on the band was history, it would be Ace and Molly out on the highway, together forever or at least until Tuesday. He resolved to spend the rest of his short life seeing what kind of trouble this feral beast woman could get him into.

He remembered an episode of *Doctor's Hospice* that Nina had forced him to sit through once. A tsunami had struck during the annual charity luau and pandemonium erupted as dozens of victims were claimed by the rushing waters. Families coming to terms with the end of their loved one's lives perished alongside beloved staff members including nurse Belinda O'Shaughnessy and her conjoined twins. As the waves finally subsided and corpses began to pile among the tiki torches, panic and dissension set in. Should they begin treating the wounded or escape to higher ground before an aftershock buried them all? Some suggested they try and sail out, others favored reviving the waterlogged dune buggies for the evacuation.

Finally, Dr. Lukas Cosgrove stepped forward and explained in a deep calmly assuring voice that the time had come for everyone to pitch in for the good of the entire team. He pledged to value everyone's input and promised that no man, woman or child who remained loyal would be left behind, finishing off by reminding everyone that winners never lose and they never ever quit.

Nina had stripped for him then, calling him Doctor and describing in minute detail her preferred remedy for what ailed her, but that now seemed like eons ago. Rejected by his band, cuckolded by his girl, and trapped in a funeral home he never made, he felt the fury building inside of him. Fuck Easy, that drug crazed little retard, fuck Birdie that four-eyed faggot and fuck Lex that big dead son of a bitch! Equanimity did not come easily to Ace Minarini. He was too dumb to be smart about things, too young to be mature about things, too petty to be big about things. A scowl darkened his face as he said-

"Nobody quits 'til it's over."

{27}

NOT DEFEAT

†

RICKY SURVEYED THE EMPTY SHELL of his childhood home, the dream of an early and prolonged retirement evaporating before his eyes. He no longer saw his future in his past or heard the plaintive call of simpler days, just the taste of a barroom floor and the smell of a legless skateboarder. He had returned to Highland Falls ready to accept anonymity, boredom, mediocrity, anything but defeat. He looked out the living room window and saw a warbler drop a mottled white turd on the Mecklenburgs' Volvo. He imagined death by carbon monoxide poisoning, though both the sporty Lexus and functional minivan had vanished.

Heart leaden, he entered the garage where only the ice cream truck remained, its happy logo mocking Ricky as he extracted his last joint and lit it, easing in behind the wheel. Pulling out the ashtray he found a note in his father's cramped script that read—

Dear Ricky,

By now you've discovered that we're dead and you're broke. We paid a truck driver to plow into your mother and me so you could collect some insurance money. You're welcome. It won't cover that reverse mortgage we got into, but maybe you can get a room downtown for a while.

This ice cream truck is the only thing we own that we didn't acquire on credit. I love this old thing. Your mother said I was a fool to buy it and maybe I was. Meanwhile, she was in love with our stockbroker, a schmuck who ran a hedge fund that bet against Goldman-Sachs! Not for nothing, but we would have done better if she'd had a crush on Bernie Madoff.

We love you, your mother and I. You're a good boy deep down, just a little lazy and shiftless. Don't spend the insurance money too fast, some of it goes to the creditors, but I'm not really sure how much anymore.

Whatever you do, don't let them bury us at that funeral home down the street. There's something weird going on over there.

> *Zei gezunt,*
>
> *Dad*

{28}

Sir Isaac Newton

✝

NINA NEVER WANTED TO SEE RICKY AGAIN, though he felt differently. When she answered the door, his heart almost pirouetted out of his shirt and smothered a bluebird that chirped in a nearby tree.

"I was gonna call, but…"

Nina was glad he hadn't called, but even more dismayed that he had shown up. After awakening to the sight of her boss spurting his last, she had dragged the body downstairs where he now decomposed quietly on the basement floor. Even for a teenage funeral director, two deaths in twenty-four hours was pushing it. The presence of this local dullard she had bedded out of sympathy last night just would not do.

"Look Richie…I have no time for you. You're not really my type of person. I don't know you, I don't like you and I'm fucking someone with a far bigger cock than yours."

Ricky had heard many and varied forms of the brush off over the years, but never one as succinct as that. He could almost have admired that level of callousness if it hadn't been aimed at him. With nothing to lose he just fired away.

"I get all that, but when you're near me…I don't care. My heart flutters like my chest is gonna burst. Ever since I laid eyes on you, you're all I can think about. I just came over to say…I love you."

Ricky Lee surprised himself with this frank admission and looked at Nina as though his life depended on what she said next. Nina thought about how she'd respond to this nincompoop online. Maybe something like-

"When you walk in the room my heart flutters, too, but only because I'm thinking, *what a fucking dipshit* while huffing airplane glue."

A smile threatened to form in the corners of her mouth and Ricky took this as a hopeful sign. He touched her cheek and they stood gazing at each other for a long moment. Then she kicked his left shin so hard that he felt it in the right one.

"Ricky, I'm never going to sleep with you again."

She dropped to her knees and took his fly down, placing his undistinguished penis in her mouth. Pain radiated up from Ricky's leg and swelled his cock. All of the love and affection welling in his heart these past few hours filled him with a feeling of invincibility he hadn't experienced since that magical summer spent deflowering the faux lesbians of Highland Falls. Nina dug her nails into his ass cheeks, absorbing his penis like a sponge. She sucked at him furiously and within seconds Ricky had orgasmed, even before getting hard. Any pleasure he might have felt, though, was mitigated as Nina hoisted herself to her feet using his nutsack like a tetherball. They eyed each other warily, panting. The high vaulted ceiling of the funeral parlor cast a majestic aura, as though something grander than the both of them beckoned.

"I'm going upstairs to wash my mouth out with carbolic acid. If you're here when I get back, I'll shoot you with my boyfriend's gun and say it was a burglary."

Nina disappeared up the staircase. Ricky wanted to follow after, to tell her again that he loved her, that he'd do anything for her. He decided to quit while she was ahead. Dejected, his head slumped forward on his shoulders like a flightless bird, he tried to find a bathroom, but the place was bigger than he remembered. Disoriented he eventually found himself at a door that led downstairs. Hesitant, unsure, but with nowhere else to go he descended.

The first thing he noticed was the corpse of the old man moldering in the center of the floor. The body had begun to harden in a strange position, as though it had given up on the idea of resting in peace. A few flies hovered nearby, but they seemed distracted, as though a body this ancient held no interest even for them. He wondered how the old guy had died. He'd seemed full of pep the day before, swinging that cane and salivating with righteous anger, but if there was one thing the last few days had taught Ricky it was that luck can turn very quickly.

He came upon an enormous walk-in freezer and opened it. The sight of five corpses in varying states of cosmetic reinvention didn't frighten him as much as the prospect of never seeing Nina naked again. He knew she'd meant those harsh words she'd said and he found the cold of the freezer bracing, the bodies comforting in their finality. One of them even kind of looked like Doris. He sat down on a step ladder and began to cry. No matter what she had done he missed his mommy. The longer he cried the harder the tears came, the ladder shuddering with the violence of his misery until a brick of cocaine dislodged from a high shelf striking Ricky's head with a thud.

If he had known who Newton was he might have stopped to ponder this one apocryphal similarity between them. Instead, he picked the chilled brick up off the floor, tucked it under his arm like an injured fullback and ran up the stairs searching for a way out.

{29}

Three and
a Half
Minutes to
Nowheresville

†

EASY RETURNED TO CONSCIOUSNESS on the helipad at Fyreball Ranch, Dr. Giddy's sprawling estate near Nashville. He didn't feel well, which is to say that he had sobered up. The only face he recognized was Birdie's. Dr. Giddy disembarked while André and Hervé unloaded the stretcher bearing Easy into the recording studio. After some half-hearted inquiries into the drummer's health Dr. Giddy got to the point.

"Gentlemen, I make records and you are going to make a hit record with me."

He let this sink in, noting the rapturous look on Birdie's face and the deadpan expression on Easy's. Birdie began to say something, but Giddy quieted him with a wave of his hand.

"I'm sure you're both familiar with the annual Golden Calf Awards presentation. Because television ratings for the show have been slipping in recent years I've been asked to create a new single over the next forty-eight hours and perform it at the GCA's just as that song is reaching peak media saturation. You are going to help me accomplish this feat and you'll be paid handsomely for it, but you must do exactly as I tell you, absolutely no questions asked. Do you both understand me?"

Birdie nodded his head vigorously. Easy stared blankly at the wall behind Dr. Giddy's head.

"It all starts with the beat, so Easy, grab some sticks and sit behind that drum kit, please. You might want some of this first."

He held out a worn cd case covered in white powder. Easy greedily snorted, then took a seat behind the kit and began pounding out a beat to warm up. Giddy's expression went sour and he snapped into the talkback mic-

"Silence! Listen very carefully, young man. Can you hear the click track running through your headphones?"

Easy nodded tentatively. He had joined his first band approximately five days after picking up a pair of sticks and the thought of practicing by himself without a loud band to cover his technique had never occurred to him. Hearing his drums all by themselves was a kind of revelation.

"Play four snare drum beats, then four kick drum beats, then on the hi-hat, etc. until you've hit every piece four times. Then get your ass back in here and don't attempt to play the drums again for any reason whatsoever."

Easy did as bidden and returned to the control room.

"Now it's your turn, Mr. Birdie. I want you to pick that guitar up and play a "C" chord as cleanly as you can, then an "F" and a "G." Then I want you to start at the lowest note on the guitar and play each note slowly until you reach the highest one."

Birdie did as he was told and returned to the control room.

"Now that you've gotten tones I guess you'll want to teach us the song, huh Doc?"

"That won't be necessary gentlemen. Are you familiar with these?" In Hervés enormous palm rested eight white pills with Xs etched across the back of them. "I'll need each of you to take four of these and have a seat on the couch."

Balzfyre didn't plan to use anything he'd recorded by the hapless pair, but he figured that in the blizzard of paperwork he'd already made them sign on route to the studio he could now claim any copyrights, publishing or artwork they might have created during their entire worthless careers. One never knew when that might prove advantageous down the line. He also wanted to be able to testify that he had, indeed, recorded the Dunderhearts (whoever they were) at some point in time. The next several hours presented a master class in hit making to a pair of young men too drug poisoned to notice. Balzfyre expertly mixed and matched beats, chords, lyrics and motifs from a half-dozen current hits creating a pastiche both new, old and frighteningly average all at the same time. Like a particularly efficient serial killer one both marveled at his talent and recoiled from the sheer vicious banality of its result.

The song that eventually emerged, *Falling Star,* told a tale of innocence lost and wisdom found in two hundred and nineteen seconds. How this unimpressive collection of clichés would ultimately encourage the outsized dreams of little girls from a hundred thousand Nowheresvilles must forever remain a mystery, though. That's because whether we like it or not, for an eternity that lasts around three and a half minutes, these tin pan stabs in the dark supply the soundtrack of our lives. If you call that living.

{30}

No Shoes
No Shirt
No Mercy

†

AS ACE PILOTED THE HEARSE DOWN the freeway toward Highland Falls, Molly hung her head out the window, speckled tongue lolling from her wide mouth like a mastiff. The last drug remnants had worn off by now and she cheerily suggested Denny's. It may have been lunchtime for the handful of melancholy diners scattered around the room, but for Ace and Molly it was still the graveyard shift. She ordered a black coffee, a Coca-Cola, an orange juice and a Rooty Tooty Fresh and Fruity breakfast. Ace ordered a burger well done, hold the lettuce and tomato. They ate in noisy silence, Ace ruminating on what he'd say to Nina when he presented this feral creature who grinned as she slurped and salivated over her food.

When the meal was done and the check presented Ace strolled to the cash register in a drowsy food coma. Molly, refreshed and rejuvenated, bounded toward the counter brandishing a twenty-dollar bill held together by scotch tape. When the register opened, she slapped the cashier so hard the ancient yellow dentures flew from her mouth. Molly grabbed a handful of cash from the drawer and ran for the exit, body slamming two unlucky Salvadoran landscapers who scattered like tenpins.

Ace clambered after her, firing up the hearse and screeching into oncoming traffic. Molly let out an enormous belly laugh and farted proudly, kissing Ace full on the mouth and leaving remnants of partly chewed pancake and artificial maple flavor across his lips. She breathlessly counted the take, announcing-

"Fuck yeah! Two hundred and twelve bucks! Score!"

Molly turned the radio on and rifled through the channels. Religion, Pop, Country, Pop, R&B, National Public, Pop, News, Pop, Pop, Country, Pop and finally, the Oldies. Tom Petty warbled, *"you got lucky babe when I found you"* and she cranked the volume until the entire car shook with it. Ace drove quickly past the filling stations and liquor stores of Mount Highland, then the malls and car dealerships of Highland Oaks and finally the upscale shops and tony florists of Highland Falls, bringing the hearse to rest in the garage under the mortuary.

Blood throbbed in his temples as Ace stepped through the doorway. He made it as far as the little room with the stained glass window before passing out cold. Molly lay down beside him and buried her face in his lap, content to hibernate on any stranger's floor.

Across town, Denny's Mount Highland location buzzed with excitement. Officers Maitland and Sandusky sipped instant cocoa and failed to comfort Denise Jagovich whose false teeth had finally been located in a wastepaper basket near the front door. Sniffling as mascara ran in clumps down heavily rouged cheeks, she described the male as over six feet with long greasy hair and brown eyes, wearing tight black pants and tennis shoes. The female was husky, loud and dirty with unkempt dreadlocks tied into a ponytail beneath a red bandanna. A curious amulet hung around her grimy neck and she wore faded bib overalls with no shoes, no shirt, no mercy.

{31}

Music as a Second Language

†

DR. GIDDY GOT GRUDGING RESPECT across the musical spectrum, from soul divas to teen queens to Hollywood music supervisors to boy bands. He'd ridden the waves of K, J and Gay Pop; Club, Street and Church House R&B; Emo, Screamo and Dreamo Rock; Regular Guy Country, Old Fashioned Gal Country and We Really Don't Like Colored Folks Around These Parts Country, enjoying massive success in every genre.

Balzfyre's hit making tool kit consisted of talent, plagiarism, bribery and not really giving a fuck about anything except sex with damaged young men. Plagiarism freed him to scour the radio dial for current hits, talent allowed him to synthesize several different tracks into a cohesive, catchy and commercial whole that couldn't be identified from any single source and not giving a fuck about anything except sex with damaged young men gave him the wherewithal to make generic art and still sleep soundly at night with the aid of very powerful tranquilizers. The bribery was done by what are known in the recording industry as 'independent promoters', broken nose types who, for a fee, pass on cash to radio, television and multimedia programmers in exchange for airplay, *vox pecunia*. It had been this way since the dawn of the recording industry where not only do things never change, but when they do, it's always for the worse.

Reality intruded fitfully into Birdie's limpid mind, his eyes struggling to focus, brain rejecting the images flashing across pinned retinas as he fought to emerge from a Rohypnol stupor that felt like swimming laps in a bright green Jell-O mold. While it couldn't possibly be true, that really did look like Easy spit-roasted between two enormous black penises while Dr. Giddy stared mesmerized through the view finder of a video camera and beat his flaccid cock raw, though.

As Birdie slept, Giddy's newest creation burrowed its way into his brain like an earwig. He already knew the song as he slept and he'd be sick of it by the time he awoke, but by then it would be too late, the track would be stuck in his head forever. Birdie dreamed about the awards show. He had always been quick to mock the GCA's as a parade of preening narcissists ego stroking each other, punctuated by mediocre performances of bloodless songs that dragged on hours longer than it had any right to. While the Oscars, the Tonys, and even the unwatchable Emmys might sometimes be entertaining in a car crash sort of way, the Golden Calf Awards were a sure fire, soul sapping, teeth grinding sleeping pill every time.

Hanging out backstage with all those good looking people basking in the incandescent glow of fame did sound like fun though. He imagined the pageantry, the manufactured pathos, the breathlessly reported backstories behind the music; imagined the breakups, the setbacks, the lessons learned, all those subtle ironies and inspiring tales of showbiz triumph designed to lure rubes like him into the music game. He saw himself in a suitably hip tuxedo, attractive female on his arm, while those who had doubted his genius looked on at home and cursed him for pulling off the impossible and making it look easy on national television. It all seemed so easy, but could anything really be that easy? Easy? What the hell were they doing to Easy...?

When he finally forced his eyelids open, Easy was dozing next to him mouth agape, the powerful whiff of anchovy on his breath. André and Hervé executed chin-ups and crunches in a corner of the studio while Dr. Giddy worked on a headphone mix for an unseen vocalist preparing to record in the isolation booth.

The next sound that Birdie heard transfixed him, piercing his temporal lobe like the sound of angels in flight. A voice at once haunting and serene, assured and dynamic, burst from the speakers like the answer to the question *"what would you like to hear every moment for the rest of your life?"*

"For Christ's sake, Bella, the phrase ends on the high note, you're going low. And you pronounced "dream" like "drahm" and "free" like "freh." I didn't realize English was your second language. Again!"

Birdie wanted to rise from his chair and garrote Balzfyre from behind with a guitar string. How could he speak to that perfect voice like that? It was like throwing spit balls at the Venus de Milo. The track animated the speakers and once again the room filled with the mellifluous euphony of Bella's gift.

"For fuck's sake, you're scooping up to that first note and petering out by the end of the phrase. Do not waste my time, I can have a Music Row demo singer here inside of an hour, please believe it. Again!"

The track lasted six seconds before screeching to a halt.

"Alright, let's just take a dinner break and try it again in an hour, for the last fucking time!"

Balzfyre rose from his chair visibly disgusted and motioned to his assistants. André picked him up in a fireman's carry and Hervé opened the door, hurrying off behind them. Sheepishly, Bella emerged from the booth, eyes downcast, tears threatening to erupt from her eyes. Birdie rose to his feet and walked toward her, focusing like a laser on this incandescent creature. A vintage Eartha Kitt hairdo crowned the face of a princess and the body of a golden age movie queen. Her skin was a shimmering onyx, her outfit understated and tasteful, a deep green choker giving her the timeless look of a pinup that could not be pinned down.

"Where did Dr. Giddy go?"

"I think he's gone for some air...Bella? That was the most beautiful thing I've ever heard. You're amazing."

She burst out crying. Birdie put a hand on her shoulder and guided her toward the sofa, attempting to sooth her as he deftly kicked Easy to the floor. She spoke softly, Birdie hanging on her every melancholy word. Eventually, the conversation brightened as she spoke of her family in Baton Rouge, the music she grew up listening to and her recent acting debut on daytime television. As they conversed, they shared a drink, maybe five.

{32}

Submission
to the
Moment

†

NINA SLEPT DEEPLY AND WOKE TROUBLED, unable even to masturbate. She rose, washed, dressed and descended the stairs half hoping that old Fredo had simply disappeared overnight. Theoretically, Minarini's advanced age made his death unsuspicious. Still, something felt amiss. Heading toward the basement she heard the familiar sound of Ace's snoring coming from the stained glass nook. By the time Nina got there, Molly had depantsed the sleeping rocker and taken his sleep hardened cock into her mouth. Ace dreamed he was a baby donkey caught in the jaws of a twenty-foot anaconda. The more his dream body melted into the gaping maw of the snake, the more excited he became. Opening his eyes to the rhythmic movements of Molly's sturdy haunches to his left, he saw Nina standing in the doorway, an amused look on her face, one delicate hand down her pants.

Molly pulled her mouth off Ace and sat down firmly on his cock, bouncing like an animated jackalope. Born to fuck, steal and be merry, she inhabited the present like a Zen master, untroubled and completely uncouth, emitting guttural sounds that only increased Nina's excitement. Molly took her time reaching orgasm because she could. Had the coupling taken place on the 'L' tracks or during the commission of a felony she might have finished much sooner, but given the situation, she figured why rush it? After all, she now had a new boyfriend and a nest egg of two hundred and twelve dollars.

Though this explosion of female id run wild looked something like a National Geographic documentary and kicked up a stink akin to the musk ox enclosure at the Brookfield Zoo, it still turned Nina on. She could see herself in that untamed creature riding her nominal beau's dick in the middle of the floor, and of all the things she enjoyed seeing, Nina still enjoyed herself the most. Minutes passed while her neurons wandered, brown gravy lapping at the corners of her brain as the writhing couple increased in carnal bellicosity. Objects began to dislodge from shelves, cascading to the floor like the desiccated shells of cicadas, their uses forgotten in submission to the moment.

Nina's ambling, epileptic subconscious glimpsed in this erotic spectacle a chance to be rid of Ace and his unlistenable rock band for good. Absently sniffing at her fingers, she walked up behind Molly's gyrating form, expertly placing her index finger on the vagabond's distended clitoris and tweaking it until Molly squirted a greasy fountain of female ejaculate toward the ceiling. Ace, now fully awake and silently celebrating the uncomfortable conversation with Nina that had just been avoided, climaxed torrentially. Satiated, refreshed and still stuffed from breakfast, he fantasized about dying right now before anything bad could happen to him. Exercising his prerogative, Ace rose majestically to his feet and ambled to the red brocade curtains, wiping his cock on one, then pissing out the open window into the decorative topiary below. Finally, he said-

"This is Molly. We need to blow town in a hurry."

{33}

Bumfuck, Wisconsin

✝

AFTER LAST NIGHT, RICKY HAD NEVER expected to see Nina again; that he stood in her presence less than a day later struck him as a minor miracle. He hadn't thought twice about rushing over as soon as she had called. Now, standing in the viewing room with its high ceilings and somber décor, he prepared for the inevitable ass kicking the pair of goons glowering next to her would soon mete out. He'd known that he would have to pay for that kilo of coke somehow. Instead, Nina pulled out the silver tray piled high with more marching powder and passed it to the grimy hippy girl who passed it to the Cro-Magnon rocker who passed it to Ricky in turn. It made the rounds twice more until they had snorted enough to cause cardiac arrhythmia. Then Nina got down to business.

"Ace and Molly need to leave town quickly. I want you to give them that ice cream truck you mentioned the other day."

Ricky didn't know what to say. That truck was the only surviving memory of his father who had loved the old thing. It represented the simple joys of an easier time, the spirit of entrepreneurship, and a last link to his dear departed dad. In a world constantly in flux it stood as a rusting reminder of his youth and of his family. And it never went anywhere quickly. He did not want to part with it, didn't even want to think about parting with it, and so he said-

"OK."

Ten minutes later, Ace and Molly didn't bother waving goodbye to Highland Falls. A green rectangular sign offered them a choice between 90 East or 90 West. In unconscious homage to Nina he chose the latter. They began the voyage by cursing the truck's fifty-eight mile per hour maximum speed and antiquated radio, but eventually they found that the ride was comfortable and Molly especially enjoyed pulling the lever that played "Pop Goes the Weasel" ad nauseum. Three hours and an entire tank of gas later, they took the exit to a town not officially designated Bumfuck, Wisconsin.

"Take that necklace off, you kook."

Molly reluctantly removed Lex's rapidly blackening penis from around her neck and threw it in the oversize ice freezer outside the Menominauck Ready Mart. Ace filled the truck with gas, checked the oil and wiper fluid and washed the windows. Molly bought Cheetos, Fritos, Tostitos, chocolate milk, four Slim Jims, a Nestle Crunch bar, two packs of Now & Laters and a half gallon of Dolly Madison vanilla ice cream; that is, if 'bought' is the proper term for stuffing most of it down the front of her overalls. Back on the road they munched in silence until Molly noticed a white puddle starting to form at her feet and headed to the back of the truck trailing creamy goo. Inside the freezer was a box of popsicles, pink bubblegum left over from the Carter administration and a kilo of cocaine.

She dropped the ice cream, grabbed the blow and rushed to the front of the truck waving the bag and screeching like a contestant on *The Price Is Right*. She pounded on Ace's shoulder making him swerve into oncoming traffic. He barely righted the top-heavy truck, screeching briefly back to his own lane and then skittering out of control and onto the shoulder three inches from a yawning drainage ditch.

"What the fuck are you doing?"

Instead of his own life flashing before his eyes, he saw Molly's life instead. What kind of fool would leave the inscrutable, delectable, amoral Nina for this outrageously retarded she-devil? It had been the Rubicon he had crossed without knowing how to spell Rubicon.

He wanted to strangle her, or better yet, have her strangle him out of his predicament. Finally, he saw the huge white sack in her hands and all thought ceased.

{34}

A Well-Regulated Militia

†

HOURS LATER, HIS UNDESERVING COCK lodged in the swanlike throat of Nina West, it occurred to Ricky that he'd stashed the stolen narcotics in the ice cream truck he had now given away. How could he have ever dreamed that the forces that control the universe would allow him to rebuild his fortunes overnight without toil and trouble? He came, then started crying, quickly stifling himself and faking indigestion. Nina swallowed, suppressing the urge to laugh for fear his ejaculate might come out her nose. Handling Ricky was starting to give her a perverse sort of pleasure. Unlike Ace, he had no confidence and no agenda. Best of all, he was average in bed, hung like a mosquito and nervous to the point of distraction so there was no danger of staying involved with him for any length of time.

"Let's go for a drive, Ricky. We need to ditch that Hearse."

Nina put her hair in pigtails and donned a plaid skirt and matching sweater. She descended to the basement, entered the corpse freezer and climbed the step ladder only to find the ready bag of cocaine missing. She assumed it must have been taken by Ace and his girlfriend, mentally writing it off as the cost of being rid of them. If she had cared enough, she might even have wished them well. Removing a crowbar from off the wall, she jimmied under the floorboards extracting three more kilos and counting the remaining bags to make sure nothing else was missing.

Moving to another corner of the basement she opened a large black cupboard secured with a massive padlock. Removing a pump action AR-15 from its moorings, she considered the Second Amendment. As far as she knew she wasn't a member of *a well-regulated Militia*, nor did she care about the maintenance of any *free State* except her own. Fortunately, no one paid attention to the first part of the Second Amendment anymore.

Nina strolled to the garage, rifle slung across her back like an indignant partisan from some long forgotten conflict while Ricky tried to play it cool. His heart beat wildly, not from the cocaine or even the presence of a loaded firearm, just from the nearness of Nina. Lacking a license or even a learner's permit, she handed him the keys to the Hearse and he slipped in behind the wheel. If they got caught, she could always blame everything on him.

As they pulled out of the driveway a glaring sun did nothing to mitigate the Midwestern chill over Highland Falls. She directed him away from the highway and toward Lakeshore Road, reasoning that it was safest to drive the hot car where the richest locals dwelled, but the pair hadn't covered two miles before Officers Maitland and Sandusky passed them going in the opposite direction. Remembering eyewitness accounts of the unique getaway car driven by the Denny's Bandits, Maitland switched on the lights and siren exhorting his partner to flip a U-turn in hot pursuit. Unfortunately for the rule of law, the flashing lights caused Sandusky to have a myoclonic seizure. He lost control of the squad car and took out four mailboxes before ending the journey in a tangle of powerlines. Studying the rearview mirror, Nina placed her small saddle shoe over Ricky's right foot and they disappeared in a puff of exhaust. The pair exited on Lakeshore Drive deep on the South Side of Chicago, thirty winding miles and a whole world away from Highland Falls.

Heading west from Lakeshore they got a glimpse of why the locals referred to the area as Chiraq, but in truth it enjoyed far less investment from the United States Treasury than any Middle Eastern hot spot. Dilapidated buildings separated by forlorn concrete playgrounds visibly moldered in the gritty sunlight. Packs of the hollow eyed warmed their hands in front of trashcan fires that stank like a dirty winter. Ricky began to get scared. He'd dwelt in urban environments for more than two decades now, but this was a part of town he had always avoided. It wasn't that he disliked black people, he just didn't know any. Still, he refused to show fear, reasoning that to die near Nina beat living without her. She told him to pull over by a cluster of young men perched in front of a boarded-up liquor store.

Keenly aware of any unfamiliar vehicle on their block, the 2-3's eyed the Hearse warily. Quickly clocking the driver as a coke desperate cracker, they sent two preteen scouts to approach the car. Ricky lowered the window, but Nina did the talking.

"We have a business proposition to speak to your superiors about."

The scouts went back to the corner, puzzled looks clouding their faces. The street is a predictable place until it isn't. Cop, shoot, cop; score, smoke, score; fight, fuck, die. Anything that throws the pattern off is considered dangerous or an opportunity or both. To the 2-3's Ricky looked weak and Nina was just some fiend's bitch. As one, the whole crew swarmed toward the hearse. Ricky instinctively jammed it into gear, his foot on the gas pedal, but Nina forcefully threw the car back into park. Ricky's head banged hard into the windshield and he slumped over, pasty tongue lolling out of his mouth. Nina exited on the passenger side with the rifle in her hands. She fired over the heads of the advancing thugs and they pulled up short, several drawing their own weapons. Nina spoke commandingly in a voice she had never used before-

"I'm going to make all of you very rich!"

It was quite possibly the only thing that could have stopped the 2-3's from firing on her, but she knew that peace wouldn't last long. She reached into the car, grabbed a brick of cocaine and tossed it to the angriest looking banger. He caught the bag, but dropped his gun which hit the pavement discharging loudly.

"Ow, fuck! You stupid motherfucker!"

The bullet had pierced the left foot of the young man on his right, who pulled his weapon and duly shot the shooter through his foot with another loud bang. Nina, sensing that anymore chaos might not work in her favor, fired several rounds into the air and held forth in her newly authoritative voice.

"There's more bags where that came from, but you need to quit pulling your dicks and take me to your leader."

She pumped the AR-15 for effect. Though the 2-3's had no idea what a cavalry was, none of them wanted it called in. Two young look outs dashed off down the street as the shooting victims hobbled after them. Nina began fantasizing about late night pizza at Medici, but decided to hold out for Lou Malnati's instead.

{35}

The Wonders
of Recording
Technology

†

DR. GIDEON BALZFYRE RETURNED TO a confusing scene
in the recording studio. Hervé and André had once again worked
their massive cocks into Easy's mouth and asshole respectively.
He hung between them like an insect pinioned between two slabs
of driftwood. For Dr. Giddy, that was the comforting part of the
tableaux.

Approaching the foggy windows of the vocal booth and peer-
ing through he became infuriated by the sight of Birdie and Bella's
heterosexual coupling. He rushed to the recording console switching on the microphones and studio monitors and filling the room
with the sounds of run of the mill sex between consenting breed-
ers. Like many things that sicken a music producer, he knew this
might be turned to his advantage in the future and so he adjusted
the recording levels to capture every labored breath, coo and sigh.
When the pair emerged minutes later, afterglow reflecting off smit-
ten young faces, Easy was back on the couch snoozing in a Rohypnol stupor and Giddy's attendants had disappeared.

"Did I say I wanted a duet?"

Balzfyre blasted the sex audio through the speakers so loudly that
Bella's ululations shook the room like the woofers in a tricked out

Impala. Bella began sobbing softly at first, continuing to gain intensity until it rivaled her own amplified love noises. Giddy turned down the volume, sensing the anger burning in Birdie's eyes, but just then Hervé and André reappeared with two pink suitcases. Bella wailed even louder.

"You've got two choices young lady. One, pick up your luggage, get lost and take this wretched little mouth breather with you. Or two, get back in that booth and sing this fucking song until you get it right." Here he switched on the sex sounds again, so loud that bottles threatened to shatter behind the wet bar. "If you choose wrong, I'll play this for the producers of that godawful soap opera you're in. Let's see how long your squeaky-clean daytime image survives that, Miss Thing."

Birdie felt his fists ball up and his jaw clenching tight. Bella touched his arm for reassurance as she headed back to the vocal booth. Daubing her cheeks with a soggy handkerchief she cleared her throat and removed a worn flask from her stocking. She took a long pull, then clamped the headphones on. Dr. Giddy said-

"One more clam and it's wipe out, Bella. I mean it."

Hervé and André flanked Birdie menacingly on the couch, while Easy slumbered like a limbless frog at a Gallic bistro. Eventually, André said -

"I just love her on *Doctor's Hospice*."

{36}

To See the Sealer

†

ROLLING AT AN ANEMIC FIFTY-EIGHT miles an hour isn't the most effective way to cross the country, but Ace and Molly drove straight for twenty-four tooth grinding hours, stopping only for gas and the occasional bodily function. The Dunderhearts had dreamed of Rock & Roll tour adventure; of sex, drugs and volatile friendships lived to a soundtrack of their own making. Now, Ace found himself rolling in slow motion through the armpit of America, alone but for a female psychopath. There were still drugs and sex, though, and that reassured him.

They had now meandered south to the I-80 freeway, that maddeningly flat and interminable expanse where the Midwest morphs into the West. After a solid day behind the wheel, Ace took some comfort in the fact that he had escaped the siren embrace of Nina West and the bloodless wasteland that was Highland Falls, the land of his birth. He took comfort in having now put three states between his kleptomaniac girlfriend and the Illinois State Police. He also took comfort in the sight of Our Lord and Savior appearing behind his eyelids to sooth and encourage him.

"Ace, I love you, my son. You are on a good and righteous path. Please remember that I am with you always in everything that you do. I am your heart, I am the truth, the light everlasting and through me you will find peace and salvation."

Jesus Christ looked much as Ace had always pictured him: long wavy hair, beard, sandals, beatific expression. Why he had chosen this particular moment to appear wasn't as obvious. Ace felt a warm luminous presence inside him, like buoyant spirit made flesh. As he pondered the Son of his Creator, he felt the truck begin to shake wildly. He opened his eyes just as he rammed through a guardrail, falling ten feet through the air to the access road below.

Molly awakened to her head slamming the headliner with such force that it banged her jaws shut and broke three aluminum fillings inserted by dentists in training at the Mattoon, Illinois Free Clinic. Ace felt every vessel in his skull explode, filling his eyes with blood and causing a dull yellow wax to ooze from his left ear. Cars honked behind them and Ace put his foot on the accelerator. He hoped that the presence of Jesus might heal the ice cream truck and guide them in the right direction, but the left back wheel had bent in the fall causing the truck to drift across lanes of traffic.

A few terrifying miles later he pulled into a junkyard and the dazed pair got out of the truck, whose bells chimed continually now in open mockery of their quest. In the distance a golden spire beckoned and Molly, pupils fixed, plodded slowly toward it. Ace followed her with his eyes, knowing he could no longer be without her, but glad to see her go. He entered a ramshackle office made from a repurposed Winnebago shell.

"I need a wheel for my truck, any mechanics around?"

"I can take a look at your truck, maybe even jimmy rig a part or two from off the lot. But I can't do nothing to bring your girl back once the dogs get a whiff of her."

Ace wheeled around to see Molly scrambling up a rusting wrought iron fence, snarling pack of junkyard canines in hot pursuit. Rushing outside he realized that he loved her, that they were going to die soon and that nothing was going to save them. Beyond the vista of detritus before him he could almost see the great hall, hear the sound and fury and feel the whole wide world tuning in via satellite. Molly perched on the gate as the junkman corralled the dogs and went in search of spare parts. Ace looked up Molly's skirt and saw heaven. She said only-

"We need to see the Sealer."

{37}

The Great Deluge

✝

AFTER RECEIVING THE HIGH SIGN from his lieutenant, shot caller Byron LeBron exited a 1963 Buick Riviera parked behind what was once a filling station. He walked slowly, head back, hips pointing toward the sky. Nonchalantly approaching the hearse, he opened his flick knife and with a deft motion sliced a neat line across Ricky Lee's left cheek. As Ricky screamed out in pain, Byron inquired as to his business.

"I'm with her," Ricky said, pointing to the girl in the passenger's seat. Byron clocked the rifle in her hands and cursed his powers of observation. He could be dead already.

"Now is that any way to start a business deal? I came here to make you rich, but if you're not interested…"

"I'm interested in who's got my crew firing rounds in the street and running around like a bunch of little bitches. Now I see, it's just a little bitch."

"This little bitch has kilos cheap if you've got the juice to make a real deal. And you look reasonably…juicy."

Nina had yet to bed a black guy. Highland Falls was noticeably lacking in them, though she had met a few in her travels. Some had lusted after her in an *at least she's white* sort of a way, but her petite form just wasn't the stuff of ghetto fantasy. Truth be told, she didn't generally find them appealing either, but something about the homicidal intensity of this particular one stirred her inside. Ricky quaked with fear, head throbbing and cheek bleeding freely on the leather dashboard. An eerie vibe of hatred covered the hearse like a fog. Even with Nina beside him, he felt like the last of the Leiber line might never leave the South Side alive. LeBron thrust his arm through the driver's side window past Ricky's colorless face, flashed a rare gold grilled smile and said-

"Byron."

Nina reached out, her hand enveloped by his enormous paw. She felt her panties turn moist. She imagined a panther so black that it wore a beret and carried a raven on its shoulder; so black that it scoured the Javanese undergrowth for menthol cigarettes; so black that if it were ever captured alive near the city of Highland Falls it could never be allowed to roam beyond the McDonald's parking lot.

"Nina. Can we speak somewhere privately?"

LeBron's cock wasn't as large as Nina imagined it, but then, nothing could have been. He took the tonguing she offered like a man who deserved it and this appealed to Nina, already growing tired of Ricky's heroine worship. Here, finally, was a man who could fuck her and leave her mangled corpse in a drainage ditch without a second thought. She wriggled from underneath him and mounted his erection, steam coating the windows of the Buick. Time seemed to suspend in the humid confines of the backseat and Nina imagined herself the captain's wife on a slave ship taking her pleasure with the human cargo. For his part, Byron had never encountered a vagina so tight and tiny. He'd fucked some white girls before, but never one with all of her teeth. Something about Nina scared him, but fear was not a useful emotion so he ignored it.

Involuntarily, Byron LeBron's mind drifted back to the puckered sphincter of Manuel, a youngster from Humboldt Park he had roomed with at Cook County Juvenile a decade before. They had been cuffed and handled and processed together; had endured cold showers and bologna sandwiches and rough toilet paper together. Finally, together, they had enjoyed an evening that no amount of Listerine could ever erase. LeBron came in a great deluge before Nina had a chance to. By some mental alchemy, that made her enjoy it all the more. Now seemed like a good time to talk business.

"I've got two more keys I can spare. I'll take $75k for the dope and this bucket in exchange for the hearse. I'll also need two powerful handguns, ammunition and three fingers in my pussy until I orgasm."

"$50k, and you know this whip got no papers, right?"

The ride back North was a quiet one for Ricky, his untreated face festering, his unknowing head throbbing. He could smell the cold funk on Nina and shame burned at his cheeks. He'd always hated the city, almost as much as he hated himself. Life with Allison was tedious, but life with Nina meant certain death.

"Look Ricky," she said, turning the Alpine up full blast and switching on the hydraulics, "it's got front, back and side to side!"

{38}

Wolverine Androgyne

✝

LAS VEGAS IS A TOWN WITHOUT PITY, but not without heart. Molly Jane Ogden felt neither pitiful nor heartless as she promised to love and honor Angelo Dominic Minarini. Raised in a rural polygamous sect that shunned modern entertainments, she had always dreamed of a full-blown Mormon wedding. True, the Honky-Tonk Wedding Chapel wasn't the Salt Lake Temple, and Ace wasn't exactly Donny Osmond, but that hadn't stopped her from choosing *Puppy Love* as their wedding march or from wearing an improvised set of white bloomers that shielded her vagina from undue cosmic influence.

Wearing the same rumpled tie and shapeless white shirt that he collected corpses in, Ace reflected on the final days of Adolph Hitler. The dapper but demented dictator had wed his long-suffering paramour on the eve of their mutual suicide. Ace saw a wonderful economy to that. Outside by the curb, the ice cream truck collected a parking ticket as the pair said *I do*. Within half an hour, in that refrigerated motel room on wheels, they were *I doing* it with dewy abandon. Ace resorted to fingers when his cocaine shriveled penis could perform no more, Molly howling like a wolverine in a bear trap.

She could no longer remember her first sexual experience, but as far as she was concerned this was her true awakening to Latter

Day womanhood. As a now sealed and committed Saint, she resolved to birth a dozen children, all of them boys, all destined to sire twelve children apiece. With a gross of grandchildren in tow she would someday lead a righteous army to the gates of Celestial Heaven, and right now she needed to get that first one percolating in her sainted womb.

Ace requested a break to try and revive his flagging member. He snorted an enormous line of cocaine, his one hundred and nineteenth since their journey began. When the drugs hit his bloodstream, his eyes rolled back in his head and everything went black, then brown, then a sort of puce with crimson swirls and maroon dots.

Suddenly, it was 1954 in the United States of America. A fedora sporting version of Angelo Minarini had just returned home to Molly and their twelve children from the night shift at a ball bearing factory. Ace was clean shaven and smiling as the whole brood, led by his youngest, Nina, greeted him at the door.

"Daddy's home," she squealed in delight.

"How's my princess today?" he asked.

Before she could answer, a stream of budding princes and princesses pelted him with affection until he collapsed on the sofa, cold Tom Collins in hand and a black, white and gray television set blaring in the foreground.

"*Doctor's Hospice* is brought to you by Lux Laundry Soap, Fab Detergent and Pepsodent Toothpaste."

Crawling onto his lap, jet black locks tied in pigtails, little Nina settled herself on his knee turning her pert nose up toward his smiling face. When his brown eyes locked on her green ones she said-

"You really fucked up this time, Daddy. You're hitched to a certified nutcase who's sure to put you in an early grave. And you could have had meeeeeeeee!"

Suddenly, her tongue was out and darting toward his genitals. He knew this was wrong, irredeemably wrong, but what could he do except stare at the television where a teenaged Nina West in bobby sox spoke belligerently to a middle-aged Nina West in gray apron and sensible shoes, black hair tied in a gingham kerchief as she struggled to get a casserole in the oven.

"I'll marry Wally or Woodrow or the whole darn tennis team if I want to and you can't stop meeeeeeee!"

While his mind hallucinated this incestuous free for all, testicles spinning like pinwheels, Ace gave himself over to the sordid pleasure of his first matrimonially sanctioned sexual experience as Molly continued to fixate on motherhood. Sensing Ace's madness descending along with her own, she felt closer to him than ever, handling his scrotum like a nest of tiny bird's eggs while a toxic amount of tropane alkaloid flowed ever closer to her heart.

{39}

Ain't
Love
Grand?

✝

ALLISON ZWEIBEL LOVED Ricky Leiber more than she remembered, but less than she loved her new job at Mitchum, Grubmann Public Relations, LLC. Work had distracted her during the initial phase of their ninth official breakup, but three months of unsatisfactory online dating was enough to convince her that it might be time to reconcile with him again. She reached for her phone and conjured Ricky, who answered sounding agitated. Had she known he had followed a sociopathic teenager to a drug market only to have his face slashed, skull bashed and ego decimated, Allison would never have made the call. But though Allison knew nothing, she did know herself. In his current state of shock and disbelief Ricky didn't even register that his speakerphone was engaged.

"Ricky, is that you?"

"Uh huh."

"What's wrong, you sound sick?"

Skipping straight to a fractious intimacy, Allison pierced his inadequate defenses. She was back in the proverbial driver's seat, he in the passenger, and there was nothing he could do about it, nothing at all. Ricky's head swam as he considered plunging out of the passenger side door and decorating the highway with his not very beautiful corpse.

"I'm OK."

Nina listened curiously from the actual driver's seat, her sadism piqued. If being cut and threatened and cuckolded hadn't belittled him enough, surely there was something on the other end of that phone that could. Ricky listened silently as Allison enumerated the faults past and present that he was expected to avoid in the future if he was lucky enough to have a future with her. Nina's amusement increased until it threatened to swallow her alabaster face whole. Sticks summarily deployed, Allison proceeded to the carrot.

"My new job is sending me to the Golden Calf Awards ceremony in LA and I got you on the guest list! Isn't that great?! It's next week so that should be plenty of time to find someone to take care of your mom."

Nina looked at Ricky, his face a bright crimson. She now knew he had lied to this woman about the reason for his return to Highland Falls and she almost envied that pit of the solar plexus feeling Ricky was no doubt experiencing when caught in that lie. It was a feeling she could not share, but then, she didn't like to share anyway. The awards show did sound fun, though. Nina had been to California before and in spite of the vacuity of its people and the oppressiveness of its climate she had enjoyed herself immensely. It was the pre-fabricated paradise where America fashioned its fanciful notions of itself and anyway, she needed a vacation from the Midwest.

Exiting the freeway at North Avenue, Nina West headed East on 90/94, back to the South Side. This jumbled confluence would bring her, several days later, to the City of Angels. Ricky, discombobulated and caught in a web of deceit and regret said-

"See you soon, Honeyboo," and hung up the phone. Four seconds later he burst into tears, wailing like a three-year-old evangelical who's just been told that one of the Teletubbies is gay. Nina listened to the sound of Ricky's sadness for what felt like hours before it trailed off into a dull whimper followed by a tormented silence. She turned to him finally and said-

"Next time you talk to your girlfriend, tell her mama needs an extra ticket to the Golden Calfs. We're going Hollywood!"

{40}

Fuzzy Navels
and
Rusty Nails

✝

DESPITE STARRING ON A POPULAR DAYTIME TV show and voicing what was destined to be the song of the year, Bella DuBois remained terminally miserable. Whether her malady could properly be described as depression, moodiness, melancholy or a dozen other terms meant little to her. Just rising each morning resembled torture while climbing into bed each night felt like entombment in a Novocain shell, the monumental weight of loneliness pressing down on her like a hot iron even in a crowded room.

Throughout her life of emotional turmoil though, Bella remained unfailingly kind. Though success assaulted her with the same ferocity that failure did, she never took it out on friends, family, cast, crew or even hangers-on. Her constant companion, her only true friend, remained alcohol. The sillier the name, taste and color the more she enjoyed it, downing clandestine gulps of Cream de Menthe and Barenjaeger, Goldschlager or Butterscotch Schnapps throughout her working day. On the set, in the studio, on planes, trains and automobiles she drank constantly, never getting surly or missing a line or cue, never emitting the telltale stink of the drunkard. When she drank, the world became tolerable, the wolves remained at bay; when she did not drink, a mournful cloud shadowed her steps. Since that last recording session, she'd been shadowed by another mournful cloud called Brian "Birdie" Kornfelter, amateur botanist and third-rate musician. She almost liked him enough to let him go, but like the Dunderhearts themselves, Birdie wasn't going anywhere.

Bella's recording of *Falling Star*, produced by Dr. Giddy, was recorded on a Sunday, mixed and mastered on Monday, delivered to broadcast media on Tuesday, posted online Wednesday and by Friday night the obligatory DJ mix was blasting from Manhattan's Meat-packing District to Stockholm's Södermalm. By the following week an excuse had been found to have Bella, as Nurse Naomi Hightower on *Doctor's Hospice*, perform the number on acoustic guitar for several leukemia ridden toddlers. Dr. Lukas Cosgrove looked on with adora-tion and lust, wondering (along with millions of viewers) how he could have jilted Naomi in favor of the wealthy (but callous) Dr. Lillian St. James (her forbidden desire to become Dr. Lawrence St. James notwithstanding).

The entertainment industry is a white whale, bloated and slip-pery, but capable of seizing the nation's eyes and ears and hence its very soul. In days, *Falling Star* had burrowed into the consciousness of fans across the globe. Once again Dr. Giddy, like an audio rapist insisting *you love it* so incessantly that it almost starts to make sense, had found the pulsing heart of popular music using only a radio, a keyboard and a young woman's gift as his toolkit.

The phone rang and Bella answered, listening intently and grunting quiet assent. Yes, she was thrilled with the new record and yes, she could meet tomorrow in Hollywood to rehearse for the awards perfor-mance and yes, she could even bring her new boyfriend and his nar-coleptic drummer along. Through a remarkable act of will Bella had stayed sober the entire week that *Falling Star* had made its assent up the charts, but Birdie could feel the boulder of her booze jones hang-ing over them both like Damocles' swizzle stick. When the call was over she shuddered involuntarily at the very thought of Dr. Gideon Balzfyre. Pulling out a step stool and reaching into a hidden kitchen cabinet for the bright blue bottle of Hpnotiq that perched there, she downed half of it before losing her footing and spilling onto the floor in a heap. Taking no heed for her own safety, she did make sure that the bottle survived the fall. After she had taken another long pull she passed it to Birdie who had rushed to her aid.

He loved her and though he couldn't carry a tune he wanted to burst into song. She could, but she didn't.

{41}

Atomic
Number Two

✝

ROUTE 66 IS A DIRTY GHOST that winds from Chicago to Los Angeles. Like Nina West's virginity it no longer exists, but rugged pioneers still attempt to violate it daily. Rolling in a Buick convertible, wide open sky above her, beaten man to her right, Nina felt strong and relentless. With several kilos of cocaine secreted in the wheel wells; stacks of cash in her purse, pockets and shoes; and firearms locked and loaded, they glided armed to the teeth with lipstick through the night.

The panhandle of Texas is not known for its cultural sophistication or imposing architecture. It could easily be mistaken for Shanty Town, Suck City or Anonymityville. But to the people who live there a tremendous pride accompanies the certain knowledge that the more things stay the same the less they really change.

Ricky Lee was a suburban boy turned man child. What he feared most, besides working for a living, was spending the rest of his days locked in domestic combat with Allison Zweibel-Leiber. The thought of it made him want to swallow razor blades. To make matters hopeless, he loved and feared Nina West in equal measure, but having been slashed open by drug dealers and now transported to the armpit of the Confederacy by her hand he had reached the limit of what he could take, even from her. Opening the glove compartment, he extracted one of the handguns Byron LeBron had supplied and placed the barrel to his temple. He turned to look at Nina who said-

"I need to take a pee."

Failing to get the reaction he had hoped for, he returned the gun to the glove box, once again resigning himself to following Nina wherever she went and doing whatever she wanted him to do. Yesterday, during the interminable conquest of Nebraska, she had decided to take the wheel without a license and he had agreed to jump into the driver's seat in case she crashed. Nina pulled off the highway near Amarillo and into the parking lot of a nondescript roadside joint whose ramshackle exterior proved to be deceptive. By the front door stood an enormous tank with the symbol *He* emblazoned on it, a copper tube jutting out the side. In contrast to its down-at-the-heels facade, its spacious interior was light and airy, the high ceiling covered in striking primary colored balloons. A sense of *joie de vivre* pervaded the place, smiles covering every warm open face that greeted the pair like long lost friends.

"Welcome to Helios, what'll you have?"

It wasn't so much the words being said, but the register they were said in, somewhere between munchkin and eight-year old at Disneyland. *He*-tender Pamela White, her tubetop a fluorescent orange, gestured behind the bar to a portable helium tank, then to the beers on tap, the wide grin never leaving her freckled face.

"Stella," said Ricky, but the bartender put a finger behind her ear in the universal gesture of *I can't hear you*. Ricky repeated his request, but Pamela shook her head, shoving the copper tube into his mouth until he'd gulped a lungful of the monatomic gas. "Stella," he said, this time in a squeaky high voice as he smiled for the first time in a thousand miles. Even Nina felt her lips curl involuntarily.

Firm but gentle hands gripped her shoulders and she found herself unexpectedly whisked off her feet and whirled around the dance floor to the dulcet tones of *Honky Tonk Badonkadonk*, that rare country song with both a sense of humor and an urban cultural allusion. Her partner turned out to be a college football hero and fraternity president named Clemson Sturgeon IV. When the dance ended he excused himself and left the bar for the night, foregoing the clumsy pass that Nina felt sure would follow the dance. Puzzled by his receding form she returned to Ricky, deep in high pitched conversation with the *He*-tender.

"You must be Nina," she squeaked, offering her the nozzle.

Nina looked around at the dancing couples and their gentle expressions, at the conviviality that young and old seemed to share in this oasis of bonhomie. Overriding her general pessimism, she took a large hit and said in her best Minnie Mouse voice-

"Ricky's not very bright, but he's trying, bless his little old heart."

Nina and Pamela White hit it off so well that after the bar closed the trio found themselves staring at the moon and a sky full of stars on her front porch. A close-and-play turntable blared scratchy records left by her grandfather D. R. "Jethro" White after he had moved on to his great reward last year. Pamela showed them the stained-glass figurines she crafted in her spare time, a little world within a world that told her story better than words ever could. Together they shared the kind of intimacy that only strangers really can; hopes, dreams, fears and obsessions bouncing off the nighttime sky like satellites.

Later that evening the three of them enjoyed adult relations, Ricky finally reliving the passions of his last magic summer so very long ago. He was not an old soul by any stretch of the imagination, the pursuit of a virtuous life held no fascination for him, the furtherance of human excellence gained via hard work and dedication always a bridge too far. But he did love a happy ending and through the unceasing wonders of carnality his gray existence once again returned to vibrant living color.

{42}

Donny Osmond
Made Me Do It

†

"...OFTEN A PATIENT MIGHT let their condition worsen rather than seek professional help in a timely manner..."

So said a doctorly voice on AM radio before the push of an ancient button replaced her with the insistent beat of what now passed for R&B. Molly manned the wheel as Ace slumbered and somewhere in the rearview mirror Wayne Newton performed *Red Roses for a Blue Lady* for the one hundred and fifty thousandth time at Caesar's Palace. The desert stretched before them like a primitive postcard, a green sign by the roadway reading "Los Angeles—208."

Then Molly suffered a massive stroke and lost control of the left side of her body. Sagging to the floor of the ice cream truck she tried to call to her newlywed husband, but no words emerged. The truck began to bob violently as she reached for the emergency brake with her good hand, abandoning the steering wheel and eliciting angry honks from cars whizzing by on either side. Ace awoke with a violent start to his paramour crouched on the floor, truck revving in a dead stop in the middle of the freeway. Half of his new wife's face was paralyzed with fear, the other half simply paralyzed. "I'm a li'l bit country...," she finally managed to grunt through the right side of her mouth, as a semi passed loudly on the right tooting its air horn in a show of long-haul indignation. Ace jumped into the driver's seat, unhooked the emergency brake, jammed the truck into gear and guided it onto the shoulder wishing that one of them had a smart phone or even a reasonably intelligent one. Molly's face crumpled while her one good eye told a story of bewilderment with a twist of resignation.

Ace knew that Molly needed medical attention immediately, by which he meant cocaine. Her right nostril hoovered the line Ace offered on the edge of his flick knife and half of her lip curled into a grateful smile that pierced his heart like a thoracic surgeon. Ace wept for the first time since the third grade. He cried for the things he'd done and the things he hadn't; he cried for his lack of ambition and complete lack of talent; he cried for the death of his bass player and his grandfather and of Lou Gehrig and Roberto Clementé. He cried without sound and without tears, but make no mistake, he cried for his wife as she lay dying, wracked with half spasms, because all he could see in his mind's eye was Nina West in all her cold, pallid perfection.

Molly's right hand groped for Ace's cock, oblivious to whom it was actually hard for. He kissed her as she freely slobbered, tasting of Flamin' Hot Cheetos and mortality. She guided his penis into the hole in her overalls and he pumped for all he was worth, their hearts racing like snakes in a hamster wheel. On the side of the highway the ice cream truck swayed rhythmically as cars and trucks rocketed past. Molly thought about Donny, then Jimmy, then Merrill Osmond as Ace penetrated her, fingernails of one hand clawing his back, toes of one foot curling in ecstasy. After she had come, he told her he loved her. Molly struggled to get up, covering Ace's face with kisses as she slumped into the empty driver's seat. With nothing left to say, Ace finished her last sentence—

"...and I'm a li'l bit Rock & Roll."

A mischievous half smile crept over her ashen face as she dipped a dirty finger into the kilo. Scooping out a chunky rock she snorted it, wiping the residue over her gums, licking half of her lips and tugging on Ace's cock for good luck. Then she opened the driver's side door and tumbled into an oncoming semi-truck in Georgia overdrive.

Fresh out of tears, Ace slid behind the wheel and put the ice cream truck back into gear, tolling its tinkling bells for his dearly departed. Fifty miles later, he turned on the radio looking for a sign from beyond. By the time he reached Baker, California sanity was no longer an option.

{ 43 }

Music Industry Functionaries Are Wonderful People Once You Get To Know Them

✝

WHEN SOMETHING NEEDS DOING in the music industry there is always a well-groomed functionary on hand to make sure lots of money and time are wasted in the effort. Brant Zessar was one such professional. Trained as an unpaid intern at Universal, he had clinched his current gig at Balzfyre Entertainment through a combination of stolen emails and clandestine handjobs that had made him indispensable to Dr. Giddy.

"Can everybody settle down please, the Maestro will be here in a minute and I just want to cover some ground rules before we get going."

Zessar started by explaining to the room full of studio musicians that in the rehearsal space direct eye contact was strictly forbidden and Dr. Giddy would be referred to only as Maestro. He then handed out non-disclosure forms binding the musicians to silence concerning Giddy's working process including, but not limited to, any sexual acts described or performed and any intoxicants consumed. Since the gig payed ten times union scale, the musicians signed the forms so quickly they got paper cuts.

Once the formalities had been dispensed with a thirty-foot hydraulic ceiling descended slowly from on high bearing Bella, Birdie, Easy and the Maestro himself, resplendent in tuxedo, assless chaps, top hat and monocle. The studio contained room enough for a symphony orchestra, but since those had been replaced by keyboards decades ago a hot tub had thoughtfully been installed where the cellos used to go. Grand entrance complete, Dr. Giddy set to work. Pointing at the drummer and bassist he dismissed them from the session, assuring them they would be paid handsomely for their lack of work. Easy then took his place behind the electronic drum kit as though he belonged there. Birdie looked quizzically at Dr. Giddy saying-

"I'm a guitar player, I don't play bass."

Giddy disagreed with the first statement, but assured him that the second one was true. Taking him by the hand he walked him toward the bass rig.

"Birdie, I'm going to pay you a whole lot of money to stand onstage at the Golden Calf Awards, but don't get it twisted, you're here to calm Bella's nerves and make sure your friend Easy keeps his cornhole open, that's all. You're a sweet boy, but you're a no talent band rat. I wouldn't let you clap your hands on any track of mine, let alone perform it on national TV. You're going to pantomime playing that bass with the amplifier turned off; the audio mixer will not hear you, the camera will barely see you and if you do anything to screw this up you'll have Hervé and André to deal with. Do I make myself clear?"

This was delivered with a pleasant smile and a good-natured pat on the bottom, but the Maestro meant every word. Pre-recorded rhythm tracks came booming through the PA and it soon became clear to anyone with ears that the new drummer and bassist were there strictly to round out the stage plot. The studio musicians, ranging from earnest young conservatory grads to somnambulant middle aged hacks, performed their parts listlessly until Bella's voice came shining through the headphone mix. By the time the first run was complete they knew they were in the presence of a singular vocal artist and some even remembered why they had started playing music in the first place. For her part, Bella just wanted rehearsal to end quickly so she could drink in peace.

"Gentlemen, you're in the presence of a star who sings so much better than you play she should be slapping every one of you with a wet towel and jamming you into a gym locker. Horns, you sound like a third-rate Tower of Power cover act; keys, you display all the subtlety of an amputee on stilts; and percussion, well I'm just embarrassed for you. Let's try it again, this time with heads removed from anuses, please."

A single tear trickled down Bella's face, but like a bansai tree falling in the woods no one saw it.

{44}

The Jerky Way

✝

THE GLITZ AND GLAMOR OF LAS VEGAS made Nina uneasy. As a general rule she liked to win things, command attention and spend other people's money; all of which were impossible when The House always won, silicone breast implants prowled the casinos and behind every corner lurked a service worker with sweaty palm outstretched. Just ten miles from the Strip though, there existed a place where sports, entertainment and senseless violence came together under a uniquely American canopy. Nestled between a WalMart the size of Kalamazoo and a cinderblock monument to dried meats called the Jerky Way there stood the Judgement Day Rifle Range. Absently sniffing his fingers and daydreaming, Ricky found a spot in the lot between two camouflage painted Hummers. He had suggested they take in a show or just relax by the pool after another marathon drive, but Nina had other plans for her first visit to Nevada.

"You got to shoot yours last night, Ricky. Now it's my turn. Stay put and keep the car warm while I'm gone."

Like America's gun owners, Judgement Day Rifle Range prided itself on being powerful and righteous in equal measure. Behind the register a calligraphed Second Amendment to the Constitution hung proudly between a sign reading: *In God We Trust, All Others Pay Cash* and a picture of the 45th President of the United States. Like the President, pretty much everything at Judgement Day was for sale.

AK-47s and UZIs; Desert Eagles and Glock-17s; custom mods for sites, stocks and triggers; ammo and camo and souvenirs; just about everything for the well-to-do citizen soldier.

They boasted all the standard firearms training courses like *Safe Shotgun Orientation* and *Concealed Carry Workshop*, but what really brought the tourists in were the various *Experiences* that gave would-be warriors the chance to use all that hardware in a simulated setting without getting hurt. There was the *Tactical Squadron Experience* for the military minded, the *Zombie Apocalypse Experience* for the cosplay crowd, the *Valentine Experience* for gun enthusiasts in love; in fact, there was a different *Experience* tailor made for nearly everyone who liked to hear things go boom. All Nina needed was some form of ID, three hundred dollars cash and a wisp of imaginary cleavage.

She chose the *Ladies Strike Unit Experience*, taught by Israeli Defense Force veteran Moishe Pippic. Though he had only risen to the rank of Corporal in the IDF, Pippic had managed to maim a Palestinian teenager who had assaulted him with saliva. Nina found Moishe somewhat attractive, while he was more attracted to the two Vietnamese call girls on temporary leave from the Palomino Club who today rounded out the *Ladies Strike Unit.*

The first order of business was a minutely detailed demonstration of the Thompson submachine gun, safety being the paramount concern of those who spew death indiscriminately on the street or battlefield. Nina had chosen that vintage weapon because it looked like something James Cagney might have used to kill George Raft in 1932. When the demonstration ended the real fun began. She imagined herself drunk on bootleg liquor, a thoroughly modern outfit accentuating her cadavoluptuous figure as she threw caution to the wind. Filling her gangster boyfriend full of lead in a jealous rage, she'd rappel down a rickety fire escape and onto the running board of a waiting Hudson Terraplane before dying in a hail of bullets herself. Oh, you kid!

"Alright ladies, are there any questions? Good, then let's get shooting!"

The weapon felt right in Nina's hands, like an extension of her clitoris. Every time a shell skittered out she felt stronger and more invincible, while the Vietnamese girls just giggled nervously every time they fired, missing their targets by a yard. Nina took aim at simulated muggers and leering thieves, clustering bullets near their paper hearts and temples, but for some reason found it harder to concentrate with the rapist target. He just hung there, fierce and menacing in a two-dimensional way, and though she felt vaguely wistful about it, she still wound up shredding his paper cock and testicles like so much nonconsensual confetti.

She fired and the world was her victim; not just angry men, but militant women and high-spirited transgenders fell like wheat to the scythe. Perpetrators black, white and Puerto Rican; Judeo-Christian, Hindu, Zoroastrian, and Bah'ai; gay, straight and just bored with the whole damn thing vaporized before her like so much pixie dust. By the time all of her rounds had been fired and the smell of warfare permeated the room, Nina's tiny shoulders ached. The unhinged look in her eyes had the hookers exchanging uneasy glances, while Moishe attempted to reassure them that they were safe in his martial presence.

With so much mock violence in the air Nina felt the urge for sex. Briefly lapsing into one of her spells she began to fantasize, panting and hooting unintelligibly the more aroused she became. Channeling her inner bonobo, she shouldered her weapon and strode purposefully toward the call girls. Guiding the young ladies to the floor in front of Pippic's feet, she unzipped his fatigues while keeping her green eyes locked on his brown ones. The hookers did as they were bidden, reluctant to argue with this armed Jezebel and relieved to finally engage in something they excelled at. Moishe knew that he had been outflanked by an amateur, but in the spirit of Aikido he allowed his opponent's force to transfer to him, resulting in two wet mouths on his cock and an immediate throbbing erection.

"Circumcised," thought Nina.

Like the only mathematics course at a community college, the young Asians took the situation in hand. Stroking and licking Moishe's manhood they soon received a load of kosher spunk over alluring epicanthic folds. Nina removed the *Don't Tread On Me* flag from a pole in the corner and wiped the girls faces off with it, kissing Pippic lightly on both of his stern olive cheeks and dropping a thousand dollars cash on the floor. She left with her head held high and three hot slugs for a souvenir.

{45}

ASPIRATIONS

†

"ALLISON, COULD YOU PLEASE COME TO Mr. Grubmann's office for a moment?"

For a desk jockey, being summoned to the boss's domain can mean elation or despair. It had been a frustrating few months since her departure from Dr. Fulbright's cozy dental practice to the front lines of Meachum, Grubmann Public Relations, LLC, where the incessant gossip and back biting left one's loyalties in constant flux. But she didn't miss the stifling boredom of her former job, and at least M&G delivered enough curveballs to keep her from falling asleep by lunchtime. Every morning she reminded herself that the Chinese characters for "dangerous" and "opportunity" were one and the same, though she didn't actually know any Chinese. Allison hadn't yet been given the opportunity to prove what she was capable of, but she was confident that given the right client and half a chance she soon would. In her aspiration journal she had even dared hope that one day the name Zweibel might ride right alongside Meachum and Grubmann across the letterhead.

"Allison, great to see you, are they treating you OK out there?"

Mitch Grubmann liked the view from behind his mahogany desk. Remaining seated he appeared taller than Allison, though she actually towered a good six inches above him, even in sensible heels. He was not a tall man, nor a thin man, nor a good man, but he was powerful after a fashion. Like a Monopoly expert pulling out victory by leveraging Mediterranean and Baltic Avenues, he had carved out a respectably sized fiefdom by concentrating his energies on Midwestern entertainment promotion. While hotshots on both coasts and Nashville got all the glory, he just soldiered on year after uneventful year watching his coffers fill. Preliminaries now dispensed with, he shared the real reason he had called this meeting with Allison Somethingorother.

"Allison, I'm going to be frank with you. Mrs. Grubmann left me recently for another woman. It's a long story and I don't want to bore you with the details, but I'm in a bit of a pickle and I'm hoping you can help me out."

Allison fingered the Mace in her purse and girded for the worst. Ever since the Time's Up movement had raised her consciousness she had been dreading a ham-fisted come on like this. Fortunately, her lawyer/cousin Jeffrey handled sexual harassment as well as worker's compensation cases. She began mentally toying with appropriate hashtags-#MeachumToo or #MannGrub or maybe even #PubicRelations.

"I know we're sending you out to the Golden Calf Awards in LA to do some liaison work and I'd be thrilled if you'd accompany me there as my personal assistant for the weekend. Now don't worry, this isn't some sort of ham-fisted pass, I assure you, you're not my type at all. I just find I'm more attractive to clients when I'm with a subordinate, one whose looks won't intimidate them. It means a flight on the company jet and a suite at the Four Seasons, what do you say?"

Without hesitation she said yes. She'd been watching the Golden Calfs on TV ever since she was a little girl, never switching channels until the award for Best Song had been given and the big finale executed. She had been looking forward to this trip for a month and the addition of private jets and fancy hotels to the pilgrimage just made it all the more spectacular. In truth, she was so excited she almost wet her pants, but she did not actually wet her pants because that wouldn't have been a good career move. Floating back to her desk, Allison dimly remembered having put someone's name plus one on the guest list.

{46}

Make America Squared Again

†

BAKER, CALIFORNIA IS HOME TO the world's largest thermometer. As Ace pulled up to the Arco station on its only commercial street he hallucinated the world's largest asshole perched atop it. Molly lay on a lost highway behind him. Ahead he saw two choices: return to Highland Falls and beg Nina to let him sell weed out of the basement of the funeral parlor or not. Not seemed like the superior choice, but then, it usually does. As the ice cream truck filled with petrol he looked up at the winter sky and the thermometer reading sixty-four degrees Fahrenheit. In front of his eyes, multi-colored dots swirled and gyrated like teenagers in a 1960s dance contest. Absently, he itched his left arm with his right hand until blood began to flow from the scraping.

"Goddamn bugs!" he thought.

Across the street stood a dozen locals in baggy shorts and red baseball caps. They were clustered around a man with a megaphone standing behind a makeshift podium. Hearing random snatches of nonsense, Ace became convinced the garbled words were aimed directly at him. Clutching a dripping squeegee yanked from a filthy soap bucket he strode across the street determined to declare himself innocent, but by the time he got there he had forgotten what he was going to say or whom he planned to say it to. He had also forgotten his middle name, date of birth and what television show the Olson twins had starred in before achieving sainthood.

"...now, more than ever, we need to keep the riff raff out and just let the rest of us make America *America* again!"

At this last phrase a lackluster cheer went up from the crowd. Like lemmings living light years from the ocean, these marginally rural folk didn't quite know where to turn for moral support these days. On television homosexuals advertised their perversions right alongside colored folks and the disabled as the Rapture bore down on the lot of them. The speech over, they moved toward their pickup trucks with a renewed sense of outrage. Ace stood directly in front of the speaker, his mouth agape as small comets and meteors danced before his eyes. Slowly, he began to clap his hands together.

"Well thank you, my friend, much obliged."

Darius Winterbottom knew a stranger when he saw one, but this one was noticeably white and seemed to have liked his speech so he gave him the benefit of the doubt.

"What brings you out this way?"

Ace hadn't the faintest clue what had brought him out this way or even what way this one was. The definitions of the words "up" and "down" were also unclear while "sideways" seemed completely impenetrable. Across the street he spotted the ice cream truck, a dead bird pinned beneath the right rear wheel. Fleetingly, he thought of Fredo Minarini and the empire his grandfather had built on corpses and sincerity. He also thought of Crispus Attucks, Frazier Thomas and Mary Poppins in that order.

"Nothing makes sense anymore," he said aloud.

Darius couldn't have agreed more. Ace's vague observation inspired a rant about the Clinton Foundation that lasted eight minutes and eighteen seconds. Ace listened with rapt attention, the smell of burnt toast lingering in his nostrils. A strong wind kicked up, blowing the red cap from the speaker's graying head and the papers containing his speech all over the parking lot.

"This damn wind!" said Darius. "It blows like hell out here sometimes."

"We really need, like, a wall or something," said Ace.

"You bet we do, young man, indeed we do!"

Finding a kindred spirit in the gas station parking lot, it felt like the Good Lord himself was working through Darius Winterbottom that morning. He invited Ace back to his place up near Mount San Bernardino to share some grub. Having eaten nothing but cocaine and processed sugar for the last week, Ace accepted with that fraction of his brain that still functioned.

The afternoon started slowly, but gathered steam with some beers, an early supper, more beers and a screening of *Hollywood Reckoning*, a low budget documentary exploring the connections between the entertainment industry, the Deep State and a plot to turn all of America's children transgendered by 2025. Ace blacked out before the surprise ending where it's revealed that the 44th President is, indeed, the Anti-Christ. He awoke an hour later hungover, depressed, nauseous and most of the other warnings etched on the prescription bottles in Winterbottom's bathroom cabinet. He washed a few down with a tumbler of bourbon and headed back to the man cave, catching the old fellow midsentence—

"...and music, you call this shit music! It was all over by the time Garth Brooks became Chris Gaines, goddamnit! The whole freaking music biz is nothing but a bunch of faggots and coons led around by hook nosed hymies so a bunch of queer ass transvestites can whirl around on the dance floor huffing poppers and sucking each other's dicks!"

Winterbottom, overcome with emotion, tumbled from his recliner onto the floor and emptied the contents of his esophagus onto a flea ridden bearskin rug. He lay there for a time hyperventilating while Ace considered his observations. He'd never actually met anybody from the music business, but that didn't stop him from hating them *en masse*, too. The Dunderhearts couldn't even get a club show in Chicago unless they presold tickets to all their friends. And they had no friends. From the floor, Winterbottom continued his rant—

"...I remember when a DJ was somebody with a radio show, not a snotty college kid with rings in his nose and goddamn pussy hair where his face ought to be, dancing around while he pushes buttons on an iPod! I'll tell you what, George Jones could kick the shit out of the lot of 'em, and he's been dead ten years or more. I'd just as soon kill 'em all and let God sort it out..."

Ace pissed and shat and splashed cold water on his face, but couldn't shake the feeling that he was still asleep, visions of Nina's revenge and Molly's demise puncturing the façade of his mental health. He didn't know where he was or where he was going, but the same could be said of every single day he'd been alive. Then a realization as cold as Lake Michigan in February chilled him to his marrow: he would never write a Broadway hit, he could barely write his name. The truth hit him like a brick to the jaw and he passed out cold, blood running from his beleaguered muzzle in a dark stream.

Ace awoke twenty minutes later and a lifetime away. Winterbottom had vanished from the floor and his front door yawned wide toward the gathering twilight. Ace stepped outside just as Darius emerged from the back of the ice cream truck, a green popsicle poking from between his lips. He embraced Ace wordlessly, then backed up two paces and saluted him before marching back inside. Pulling out of the dirt and gravel driveway as darkness fell Ace could still taste the Rebel Yell whiskey and Hot Pockets that swam in his stomach like microwaved turds in an acid punchbowl.

It did feel good to have someone to talk to, even if just for the afternoon, and it appeared that his new buddy had even left him a parting gift. Ace gunned the engine, but paused at the end of the driveway, turning around to examine the huge pile of assorted armaments that Darius Winterbottom had insisted he would need for the mission that still lay ahead.

{ 47 }

Downtown
Los Angeles
is a Sewer
with Sunshine

✝

AS SPORTING ARENAS NAMED AFTER office supply chains go, the Staples Center is a lovely place. Nestled in a neighborhood that rivals Detroit for being dangerous, culturally barren and well-nigh deserted all at the same time, Staples sums up the current state of the music industry like nowhere else. New York used to host the Golden Calf Awards occasionally, they even tried Las Vegas once, but this celebration of comically oversized egos that come and go in a weekend could only truly belong to the City of Angels.

Limousines lined the parking lot like sleek black vultures, disgorging the wailing corpses who made the whole world sing. Country singers tried to appear authentic and approachable surrounded by bodyguards with headsets on. Rappers rode in stretch Hummers sporting enough bling to impregnate a thousand inner city teenagers. Rock stars clad in tuxedos with tennis shoes worked ubiquitous smart phones making sure their wayward agents, managers, lawyers, publicists and hangers-on didn't take the night off. These driven, overappreciated artistes simply couldn't rest easy until everyone who had doubted their vision had been made to suffer for it.

When the limo bearing Bella, Birdie, Easy and Dr. Giddy pulled up, Hervé and André ushered them onto the red carpet. A pale imitation of Joan Rivers buttonholed Bella, expressing love for her new song, her outfit and her daytime acting prowess. Bella smiled gamely, silently thanking God that she had remembered to refill her hip flask as they pulled in. Birdie, dazzled by the flashbulbs and hype, loomed at her side, equal parts proud, pouty and petrified. This business was killing Bella and after tonight he'd have a few choice words for Dr. Gideon Balzfyre, but that would have to wait. Drunk and high as an Afghan kite he prepared to go onstage like a fraud and pantomime the bass part to a song he had heard a thousand times and now hated more than Disney's *It's a Small World After All.*

Easy, mollified with cocaine and booze, wafted like a cloud through the spectacle. True, his dreams had been a bit disturbing since blundering into Dr. Giddy's orbit; but you couldn't argue with free drugs and money and tonight he was going to get paid to be on TV! Rock & Roll heaven suitably attained he could now die happy or oblivious, what difference did it make?

"Dr. Giddy, you're up for five awards tonight including Record of the Year! On top of that, you've just produced a worldwide smash that your newest discovery Bella is performing live onstage for the very first time at the GCA's tonight! Can you tell us how you feel?"

Balzfyre began to formulate a generic reply, but before he could utter it another more militant questioner intruded onto the red carpet clad in a Time's Up T-shirt and vintage Angela Davis hairdon't. Pushing the other interviewer aside she thrust a microphone in the producer's face—

"Dr. Giddy, any comment on your arrest in a Thai brothel last year that caused so much furor at the American consulate? How do you feel about those sexual assault allegations lodged against you by Zenobia the transgender R&B diva?"

Gideon Balzfyre had no use for the media if he wasn't creating it himself and he especially loathed awards night scandal mongers posing as the puff press. But he'd been bushwacked enough over the years to know that only by returning the conversation to music could he turn the tables on the tiresome party poopers who had heckled him since his career began.

"How do I feel?" he asked rhetorically. And then he sang loudly in a low mournful basso that seemed to well up from the soles of his feet—

"Sometimes I feel
Like a motherless child
A long ways from home..."

{48}

A Short Happy Life

†

THE DRIVE FROM INLAND SOUTHERN California to Hollywood is as much metaphorical as spatial; the high desert like Alaska with sand, the city like Paris without elegance or charm. An evening spent amassing firearms and stuffing his head with conspiracy theories now had Ace reaching for the radio dial to soothe the wild beast within. He found cold comfort there.

The wailing of country singers describing their exurban existences suddenly filled him with a seething rage. To hell with your pickup truck, your cabin by the lake and that longsuffering little lady that stuck with you through all the drinking and carousing. There was nothing genuine about them but their boots and despite the countrified twang, these good ol' bros seemed to define the phrase "all hat and no cattle."

Switching stations, he was assaulted by a nasal tween admonishing her boyfriend to get his act together or hit the road. No sooner had that number faded then another snotty little cash machine intruded on his eardrums, sounding as sincere as a used condom salesman as she droned listlessly over a backing track that had started life as a sample taken from a drum machine and diminished with each atrocious repetition. Every station yielded fresh outrages. R&B singers sang heartfelt tributes to imaginary lovers while wringing a half dozen appalling flourishes out of every syllable; Mexican mariachi bands drew from a junkyard set of mismatched instruments including accordion, harp, guitarron, violin and avocado; college stations blared backpack rap encouraging the ghetto to come together and fight the oppressive powers that held them down while bragging unironically about shooting "niggas."

With each turn of the dial Ace grew angrier, his disgust climaxing to the soporific sounds of public radio. An insufferably languid announcer introduced the inspirational story of some visually impaired gender fluid singers called the Blind Boy/Girls of Louisiana, nominated for Best Alternative Gospel Record of the year. Why God used so many blind people to spread The Word had always eluded Ace. Why couldn't He use the deaf and dumb instead? Their misery was certainly biblical enough.

Searching for a gas station, Ace exited the freeway in downtown LA and slowed to a crawl in traffic near the Staples Center. Presently, the ice cream truck got diverted to a back entrance available to commercial vendors only. He parked among dozens of food trucks representing a United Nations of unhealthy cuisines. Ace began to feel flush all over, as if hot tar were running down his back. He tore off his socks, shirt and pants while moving to the back of the truck and pulling out the half-depleted kilo of contraband. Sticking a greedy finger, then a whole hand and then two inside, he scooped the powder down his throat and up his nostrils until his face gleamed a dull pinkish white. The voices blaring in his head had now drowned out all rational thought.

Head aflame and body tingling he fell to his knees and reached for the metallic sky of the truck. Nina was lost to him; Molly had suffered, died and was two dimensional; Ace knew he had squandered suburbia's salvation. But while there was no hope left for him or the Dunderhearts, he could still sanctify his wife's demise and save her phantom brood of pint sized Ninas; he could still make manifest Mollie's Latter-day dream and emerge fortified like a caterpillar shedding its skin to find the butterfly within. Ace turned his face upwards slowly, smearing the bag of cocaine over his entire body and becoming one with the ancient Incas. Tonight, he would sacrifice them all.

As he ruminated on the end of the world, Angelo Minarini felt happy for only the second time in his short life. The first was when he had placed his penis inside Nina West. For that one shattering moment he had felt that life was indeed worth living. Now, with Los Angeles shimmering like a stricken movie set in the background, he felt equally elated that death was worth dying.

Mechanically, he donned the crisp white costume that had lain unworn since Morris Leiber had bought the ice cream truck decades ago. He filled a large metal freezer box with explosives, guns and ammunition, topped it off with a box of popsicles and strapped it over his chest. Placing a creased white paper hat on his head and exiting the vehicle with an armload of trouble, he followed a flock of worker bees toward the backstage entrance. Providence and his own sticky fingers soon supplied him with the vendor's ID he'd need to get past the Neanderthal doormen and meet his destiny.

{49}

An Ass Kiss Orgy

†

ROSS ASHER GRUBMANN DIDN'T actually own the jet that he bedded Allison Zweibel on, his company leased it for tax purposes, which made the blowjob and concomitant ass tonguing that much sweeter. Coming in her hair, he reflected on the intersection of money, fame and attractiveness that inclined homo sapiens to mate with each other, then search for excuses. After the orgasm, he wished that Allison might transform into a steak sandwich, light on the onions, extra provolone.

Landing on a private strip at Long Beach Airport, his lust long since sated, Grubmann imagined scenarios whereby he might snatch Bella DuBois' PR contract from the infuriating maw of Beachum, Mandlemann, LLP; Hollywood schmucks every last one of them, looking down their noses at Midwestern rubes like him. Perhaps he'd casually mention the allegations of inappropriate contact between Mandlemann and his last five assistants, two of whom now shared a house in Bel-Aire with the proceeds from their harassment claims. Allison, strolling the well-appointed aisle of the jet and imagining more affection than actually existed between them, bent down to kiss Grubmann. He flinched visibly.

"Ross, this is incredible, I can't believe we're here already. Isn't it exciting!"

Maybe for her it was, but Grubmann needed to be free of encumbrances tonight if he really hoped to poach some illustrious clients and convince a more attractive woman twenty years his junior to sleep with him.

"Let's keep it professional, Allison, there'll be lots of past, present and future clients in the house tonight and the last thing we need is a scandal. Just call me Mr. Grubmann and keep a discrete distance while we work the room. Watch and learn and good things will happen for you soon, I promise."

Allison contented herself with this reply. Ever since clearing Illinois airspace she'd fallen in conditional love with Ross, determined to become the next Mrs. Grubmann through sheer force of will. Someday, he'd see that glittery young things didn't have the staying power she did. As their Town Car slid into the gathering LA twilight, Allison took a moment to gloat. Backstage at the Golden Calf awards, Gulfstream jets, love in the stratosphere, it was all too much! What Ross could teach Ricky…

Oh Christ, Ricky! Had she really invited him and his ailing mother to the GCA's? What was she thinking? For years she'd let that sad sack smother her dreams. Now, because of a phone call during a fleeting moment of loneliness she might be backsliding into misery again. She prayed that Ricky dropped dead of a mysterious illness in the next two hours and resolved to ignore his increasingly pathetic texts until she was back in Ross's arms again.

After an awkward limo ride and the requisite round of *don't you know who I am!?* with security, they were backstage. Grubmann, pursing his lips unconsciously as he prepared for the orgy of ass kissing ahead, ditched Allison as quickly as he could. No sooner had he made his exit than Ricky, in disappointingly casual wear, turned the corner. Face to face with his ex, he felt as though he'd glimpsed the errant mark on his permanent record. He moved tentatively to hug her even as she radiated a frigid body language.

"How have you been?" she asked, not caring.

"Great," he said, thoughts of suicide gnawing at the sides of his brain.

"I've been so slammed, they've got me setting up interviews and photo shoots and lining up meet and greets and schmoozing with the artists. It's a lot of work, but it's fun, too…"

She trailed off, but Ricky had already assumed the eye rolling demeanor of a husband who would gladly surrender his left testicle if it meant removing his wife's voice box as well.

"What Nina could teach Allison," he thought.

"Where's your mom at, anyway? I'm surprised she wanted to come, this doesn't really seem like her kind of scene, y'know?"

Ricky said nothing, feeling the familiar disconnect that shared domesticity aroused in him. His intellect had ceased to function, his heart just a mass of thorns and briars, his guts a vacuum of fear and trepidation. He never wanted to see this woman again, but he didn't want to die alone. For several long seconds Allison considered her ex with his mouth agape, his shoes untied.

"I really better get back to it though, there's a million things to do here, really great seeing you…"

Allison spotted the star of *Doctor's Hospice* walking by and wondered if her ex-boyfriend could be euthanized mercifully.

{50}

Sentimentally Retarded

✝

NINA FELT LOST IN THE CONCRETE immensity backstage at the Staples Center. It almost made her appreciate Highland Falls. Two contest winners, young glamorettes in ill-fitting evening wear, careened down the hallway, mouths aflame with information gleaned from the internet and the super market checkout stand. *Oh my God! Wasn't that the guy from Generica with the ex of that guy from the Baphomettes? He cheated on her until she found out and left him for the nanny, but she turned out to be bulimic and got their kids hooked on laxatives...*

People she almost recognized from television strolled by, eyes glued to their phones. When they chanced to look up, they appeared confident in that way that only famous people with just a smattering of talent can. Nina wanted to meet them, but only to make them suffer. Famous musicians passed by as well, but Nina didn't know who they were. Why just listen to music when looking at things on TV was so much easier? She had tolerated Ace partly because he couldn't actually be called a musician. That, and she liked the way he smelled after rehearsal. She couldn't help but wonder where he and his walking disaster of a girlfriend were right now, feeling reasonably sure it wasn't the library or a volunteer fire department. She did miss him a bit though, chiding herself for even that rare glimmer of sentimentality.

"Excuse me, don't I know you? You're from Chicago, right?"

"Highland Falls."

"Aunt Mimi's funeral! You helped with the service at Minarini's place. What brings you out this way?"

The inquisitor relished fucking celebrities; sometimes he fucked them out of their money or their reputation, but occasionally he just plain fucked them. And though she wasn't yet famous, Nina's comely physique coupled with the sudden appearance of his subordinate Allison rounding the corner at the opposite end of the hallway inspired him to swift action.

"How would you like to meet a giant in the country music field, Miss…"

"Do I have to?" she asked as he guided her toward a dressing room a few doors down. Inside sat a somber looking gentleman somewhat north of sixty years old. His stars and bars belt buckle caught the fluorescent light, juicy plug of chaw bulging in his right cheek. He looked first at the girl and then at the fawning toad rushing to shake his hand.

"Mr. Ormous, Mitch Grubmann. I used to do radio promotion for you once upon a time…"

Dixon Ormous didn't recognize Grubmann, but he did know a Jew when he saw one. Instinctively, he checked the stranger's skull for horns. Since the death of his more tolerant brother, Coxon, he had realized that life was both short and precious. Dixon felt he had too little of it left to spend in the presence of kikes, spades, wetbacks, faggots or fake-titty harlots, which seemed to be all they really had here in Los Angeles except for manufactured earthquakes and forest fires.

"I do not recall you, Sir, and I'll ask politely once and one time only for you and your daughter to leave me in peace."

Ormous, perched on the specially ordered porch swing his representatives had insisted be installed in his dressing room, reached behind it and extracted a vintage Winchester Liberator rifle. He pointed it at Grubmann's paunch, reasonably sure that this Semite had voted for Barack Hussein Obama twice.

"Oh, she's not actually my daughter, Sir…" said Grubmann before catching site of the firearm, turning on his Giacomettis and exiting the room so quickly he might have been a cartoon. Nina looked calmly from the rifle to the man holding it and then back to the rifle again.

"Double action striker fired? Nice."

{51}

The Hole
Behind His Eyes

†

BEARING COLD TREATS ON A HOT Southern California night made Ace very popular backstage at the GCA's. Beaming faces, tongues coated in rainbow colors, melted before his eyes as he worked his way through the labyrinth; his mind continuing its spiral toward madness. Yet he radiated the calm that comes from being needed, wanted and loved, if only for the moment. The icebox, weighed down with munitions and frozen desserts, felt light around his neck.

"Ice cream man? Can you come this way please? The air conditioning's off in this room and I think the band could use some refreshment."

Entering the tropically sweaty dressing room of alternative rock superstars Jellygazer, Ace saw his own band in a funhouse mirror. The drummer sat in a corner quietly warming up on practice pads while Buddhist chants played in his headphones. The bassist perched on a yoga mat in the lotus position, the spiritual guru next to her standing on his head and fingering a chunk of hematite crystal while reciting the Sanskrit alphabet backwards.

Ace entered the room and an uncomfortable silence ensued. Ironically, Jellygazer's debut record *Uncomfortable Silence* had just been certified platinum. This year's blockbuster major label effort, *Emotions Empowered,* had snagged eleven Golden Calf nominations vaulting the group to worldwide acclaim. Still, a brooding sadness permeated the room as though no amount of notoriety, wealth or adulation could fill the void left by parents who had loved the sensitive souls of Jellygazer far more than they deserved.

Ace reached into the ice box pulling out popsicles with both hands and eliciting a horrified gasp from the Jellygazer collective. One waif-like creature, clad in magenta unitard and beret, ran screeching from the dressing room. As one, the band and their entourage aimed withering glares at Ace; fingers pointing, they began to chant in unison *shame, shame, shame*. As the noise grew the GCA functionary who had brought Ace into the room quickly exited, fearing for his job.

"Anybody want a popsicle?"

Ace unwrapped an orange one and began to suck at it to cool the fiery hole behind his eyes. He'd all but abandoned his Rock & Roll dream, but in Hollywood dreams die hard. Surveying the candles, yoga mats, minerals, kombucha tea dispensers and North Face Micro Yurt adorning the dressing room, he began to feel dizzy, weaving on his feet as a piercing noise broke through the din between his ears.

Rising phoenix like from the floor while blowing an amethyst encrusted rape whistle, left eye crying a perpetual tear, Jellygazer's lead singer made his/her/their presence known. Wyndan Moore had grown up on the not so mean streets of Malibu, an hour from downtown LA, but a thousand miles as the raven flies. They sauntered toward Ace Minarini looking like the cat who swallowed the canary shaped macrobiotic tofu. A mischievous glint in their eyes, one green and one blue, matched the color scheme of their skirt and poncho ensemble. Taking the popsicle from Ace's hand and regarding it as one might a Bangladeshi leper begging for change in Times Square, they spoke softly and carried a small stick.

"I just hope you're satisfied. You've driven Sascha from the room, Calliope is about to burst into tears and poor Ariadne has fainted in the corner. You smell like a barnyard, your little freezer box is wreaking havoc on the yurt's humidity control and this…this diabetes flavored projectile you're waving around is an abomination!"

Multiple facial piercings blazing, they took the offending frozen confection and hurled it against the wall, their whole posse simultaneously thrilled and petrified at this awesome display of power. Moore stood proudly before Ace, thrilled by the inevitable violence the unenlightened always meted out to their moral superiors. He could almost feel those rough hands around his throat, choking the virtue out of him.

But Ace just continued sucking vacantly at another popsicle, his mind wandering to the image of Molly perched among the clouds gazing down on him with a covey of jostling ankle biters at her feet and stars where her eyes had been. Naturally, the faces of her children were all Nina West: Nina in pigtails and party dress; Nina in graduation robe and mortarboard cap; Nina in color, black and white and ultra violet. Lost in reverie, minutes ticked by as Ace mentally explored his dual paramours; Molly and Nina, as different as night and late night. Both were strong, proud and fierce, but one of them was dead and one would never, could never die. He was free of them now, as free as a jack-in-the-box imprisoned in a wooden crate until he popped with the force of a windup clown.

By now, Wyndan Moore had assembled Jellygazer, their spiritual advisors and significant others into a circle in the center of the room to perform their pre-performance ritual. They began by invoking the moon goddess, beseeching her for the wisdom to bring mindfulness and docility to all sentient beings.

"Luna, we beg you for the strength to be weak in the face of hostility, to be soft in the presence of hardness. We pledge to balance our yin and yang, but especially our yin; to seek your blessed harmony, never letting bellicose testosterone overrun nurturing estrogen in pursuit of our communal dreamscape..."

Ace felt a shudder run through him, as if a popsicle had been inserted into his heart. Behind his eyes a snap, crackle and pop of blood vessels burst like aerosol cans in a microwave oven. He removed a modified semi-automatic Glock 9mm pistol fitted with silencer from the ice chest and murdered everyone present in the coldest of blood.

{52}

Spare Me
Your Theory
Alien I Am
Creator

†

SITTING ON THE OLD-FASHIONED PORCH swing in Dixon's green room, glass of sweet tea in hand, Nina felt like a part of history, a subject she had no interest in. Ormous bloviated at length on the threat posed by caravans of shiftless migrants, fluoridated water and the dome that stretched over the sky beyond which only the Almighty Father, the Son and possibly Tennessee Ernie Ford could travel. He stunk like a potpourri of halitosis, chewing tobacco and Dr. Bronner's soap.

"...if the coloreds want to vote why don't they admit that they started the Klan in the first place just so folks would feel sorry for 'em? God knows the Jews administer the elections anyway and if they could build the Egyptian pyramids, why can't they handle a few rock throwing towel heads in Gaza for Christ's sake? They already control North America, the banks, the movies and the National Parks, that's why there's always a forest fire in Californy, so the bankers can lend the government more money to pretend to put them out. And then there's a mudslide and before you know it they've emptied the Federal Reserve like they've been planning since the Old Testament..."

The idea that the deep secrets of the Illuminati were known only to those with gun racks and double wide trailers seemed implausible to Nina. This kind of conspiracy twaddle set her teeth on edge. She had never been discriminated against and the only minority she really felt a part of was the physically attractive minority. More importantly, as unimpressed as she might be with modern music, she knew that without blacks, Jews and homosexuals she'd be stuck listening to songs about pickup trucks and the flag. She thought again of Ace, Lex and the rest of the Dunderhearts. Sure, they were dumb, but harmless except to themselves. They spent their time getting high, chasing girls and occasionally playing music, not looking for scapegoats.

"...mark my words, pretty soon you'll have full grown adult transvestites posing as females infiltrating junior high schools just to get a gander at some teenage poontang, pardon my French. It's a question of man parts and lady parts and never the twain shall meet. I heard about some faggotry going on mid-ships in the Merchant Marine during the Vietnam era, but ..."

Nina's mind began to drift, her spell descending like wet clouds across the hippocampus, the shadows of blackbirds sauntering across a crimson sky. Ormous's twaddle hummed like a cross burned on the lawn of a foundling home. Down the corridor came a bright piping laugh like a whippoorwill high in the lonesome pines. It was a kind, gentle and understanding laugh, one that had seen its share of adversity, but had emerged stronger despite the ravages of time. Ormous' face abruptly morphed from world weary scowl to expectant grin at the sound of his beloved wife June.

"Thar she blows, young lady, that's the sound of my contentment. No matter where I roam, when I hear that merry chortle I know the little woman can't be far behind me. She still makes this old heart flutter, fifty-one years since we met on the set of the Louisiana Hayride. I'll never forget that evening, a harvest moon hung in the sky..."

Nina returned to mundane awareness, touched by the old man's love of his wife. It seemed simple, yet profound and even magical.

She wondered if there would ever come a day when someone might speak of her that way, though she couldn't possibly reciprocate. As the laugh moved down the corridor the old man rose to his feet removing his Stetson, a beatific smile on his face. Nina quickly pulled his zipper down, yanking both his pants and a partially full adult diaper to the floor. His shriveled penis hung like chewing gum from the bottom of a weathered oak desk. As June Ormous entered the room trailed by her cackling entourage they were treated to the site of Nina West, her hair a mess, lipstick smeared and Dixons' manhood flapping in the air-conditioned breeze inches from her face.

"He made me do it! He said he'd call the orphanage and report me if I didn't! He promised a bus ticket home and money for some food, I haven't eaten in three days, please don't send me back there, please, they beat me something awful when I misbehave…"

"Goddamn it," thought Dixon. "I knew she was a Freemason!"

{53}

Back In Style

†

RICKY WALKED THE BACKSTAGE corridors of the Staples Center lost and confused. Ever since Nina had sauntered into his life with that inscrutable demeanor and perfect little ass he'd felt compelled to do as she commanded, but no matter what he did, she did not care. As for Allison, he loved her he loved her not, she'd call or she wouldn't and he'd always answer the phone when she did. He had hoped that complete surrender to Nina might somehow negate perennial retreat from Allison, that somehow one would evaporate in contact with the other. Instead, only his antiseptic suburban fantasy had dried up and blown away. There was no home to go back to, no woman to run away from, only Nina the uncaring and unreachable, looming before him like an exam that couldn't be passed taken in the midst of another school shooting that couldn't be stopped.

"Ricky Lee, is that you?"

Fabian Lovejoy always landed on his feet. Veteran of a dozen nowhere bands, he somehow soldiered on, a permanent smile on his face and coins in his pocket. He might have been nineteen or ninety in clothes that came back as retro even as they went hopelessly out of and then back into style. He'd made fast friends with Ricky and a hundred other Ricky's over a lifetime on the road, his optimism still radiating undiminished.

"What brings you to Tinseltown, hombre?"

Ricky really didn't know, but stammered something about needing a change of scenery. It turned out that Fabian had landed a gig as the token white keyboard player in a British reggae band. They had scored an unexpected hit with an island flavored cover of *Yummy Yummy Yummy (I Got Love in My Tummy)*, an American bubblegum standard guaranteed to make Peter Tosh shift uncomfortably in his grave. The song had been featured in the wedding scene/food fight of a popular romantic comedy currently storming the cineplexes and once again Fabian was riding high in the dirty business of dreams without really doing anything. Bob Dylan once observed that when you've got nothing you've got nothing to lose. He might have been speaking of his own vocal cords.

"Dude, you should road dog for us, we need someone to roll joints and wrangle drink tickets out there."

Fabian's group, Dread Chuffed, had just performed at the Golden Calfs, but couldn't stay for the rest of the ceremony. They had to get in the bus and roll all night to Reno for a 420 Fest tomorrow afternoon, then it was on to Colorado Springs and Santa Fe, Cheyenne and Omaha, Des Moines and then Peoria, Illinois. Fabian offered Ricky the tour manager's job: three months solid, twelve hundred a week and all you could smoke. It sounded like heaven to Richard Leiber, the last of his name.

"If we're leaving right now, count me in!"

The music business is a heartbreaking waste of time, but it sure beats working.

{54}

Spirit Animal:
The Vixen

†

"DR. LUKAS COSGROVE?"

"Lance Middleton. I'm not a real doctor, I just play one on TV."

Nina West had no family to speak of, no friends to count on, no scruples to guide her through this life. But she did have *Doctor's Hospice*. Raised in the rarefied air of Highland Falls where young ladies dream of marrying real doctors, Lukas Cosgrove loomed larger in her psyche than Christ had for Joan of Arc. Tall, dark, handsome, rich, smart, caring, adventurous and open minded, he was everything she could want in a fictional character. Now here he was in the flesh.

"Doctor, I've been experiencing a burning sensation deep inside and you're the only one who can heal me."

She took him by the hand and led him into an empty dressing room, lust overtaking her like fire ants on a rotting donkey. Middleton took it all in stride, muscles relaxed beneath bespoke Kiton tuxedo. While this type of thing didn't happen to him every day, it did happen about once a week.

Nevertheless, when Nina kissed Lance Middleton for the very first time, eyes closed and toes curling, he felt a seismic shift inside. Bachelorhood had served him well, but then everything always had. He hadn't realized that a gaping hole dwelled in the very pit of his being, but the longer that kiss lingered the more obvious the cure for it became. Moments later he surrendered. For her part, Nina claimed Dr. Lukas Emil Cosgrove (sic) from here to eternity, allowing of no rivals or pretenders to his phallus.

She dropped to her knees and engulfed the imaginary surgeon. Middleton lit a hand rolled cigarette laced with Moroccan hash, striking a blue tip match to the snow-white part in Nina's hair. She felt the heat of his hands as she slurped gleefully at his trough, quickly taking a mental inventory of past penises and finding them all wanting. To Nina, Cosgrove's manhood presented an opportunity both to sup and to nest, a place to channel her spirit animal, the vixen.

"Hollywood is a wonderful place," thought Nina.

Lance Middleton parried and thrusted with admirable dexterity. A strict regimen of yoga, organic paleo diet and tantric sexual exploits had prepared him for Nina's exceptional genitalia, that much was true. But it had not prepared him for the perfected rest of her. Trapped in her steaming teen orbit he succumbed to that atavistic force that is Nina West. Accustomed to instant gratification, he somehow wanted this moment to last forever; spoiled beyond his talents, jaded beyond belief, still he fell under her spell and began to picture himself growing old with her while she remained forever young.

{55}

Somebody
No Everybody

✝

LI'L MAPLE COULD NEITHER RAP NOR sing and dance. He didn't actually write his own songs or produce them either and his average looks meant he couldn't even just stand there looking pretty. In fact, his complete lack of talent, wit or substance was made manifest in every agonizing moment he occupied the stage. He was also the world's most popular entertainer. Penetrating the media circus at age fifteen as the sympathetic cripple in a Canadian soap opera, his improbable rise to the top of the rap game had occurred due to canny management, dumb luck and an audience that no longer knew any better. While his handlers worked overtime figuring out tax avoidance strategies for his LLC, dance floors worldwide churned with his middling tracks and exhortations to party all night long. At last count twelve of the top ten hits wore his name and soft drinks, shoes, snowboards, parkas and thongs alike bore his distinctive maple leaf cannabis logo, a tribute to the power of positive branding. Now, with pop chanteuse Duchesse by his side, he strode to the podium to introduce Bella.

Duchesse had gained acclaim in her teens stringing lines of abstract poetry over generic DJ beats. Her very first hit *Regals* used words chosen at random from a thesaurus by her toy pug Sprinkles. Now aged twenty-one, her current work expressed that dissatisfaction felt only by those who have everything and think they deserve it. The vague nature of her lyrics caused one venerable old music mag to describe her as "seminal and important", while a newer multimedia site gushed that her work, "perfectly captures the zeitgeist of Generation Z". Duchesse had defied the odds for female performers and was still considered relevant even after sprouting pubic hair. Together, she and Li'l Maple represented the very best that the commercial music industry could muster in the year two-thousand-and-twenty.

"And now, performing her smash hit *Falling Star* please welcome to the stage…Bella!"

In spite of itself, the industry still produced some bona fide geniuses and Bella certainly qualified. Endowed by her creator with a pristine musicality, rapturous applause filled her ears with a joy that deadened by the time it reached her brain. The exhilaration of singing with friends in church had long since been replaced by a dull wish to please the powers that be and then flee to the safety of her addiction. As the introduction kicked in she looked around at the assembled glitterati, so very different from her people back in Baton Rouge, and she wanted, she needed, she would kill for a drink.

When Dr. Giddy gestured grandly toward the band she began to feel light headed. The autopilot that switched on whenever she performed had worked flawlessly for years, but now it simply failed her. She missed her vocal cue, then heaved a great milky load of vomit on the stage in front of her, viscous strands hanging from frosted lips as her knees buckled. Before she hit the floor, Birdie was bestride her sweeping her tiny frame into his arms and cradling her large telegenic head.

Giddy's first reaction was fury that this pathetic lush had ruined his TV performance, but soon his media savvy kicked in. He hurried across stage toward Bella trying to appear concerned, reasoning that a show of compassion here might convince Interpol to back off on charges currently pending against him in Bangkok. Bella went limp in Birdie's embrace. He looked up, searching for help, pained expression causing delight among the paparazzi hoping to capture an iconic moment of misery amidst all the show biz puffery.

It was then that Ace, standing stage left, face dripping with popsicle juice and narcotics, unloaded five bullets in the direction of

Dr. Gideon Balzfyre. One bullet ended Dr. Giddy's life, the other four hit bystanders, one of whom belonged to the National Rifle Association. It's often said by those who value circular disputation that guns don't kill people, people do. What is indisputable is that bullets kill people. Sometimes they maim, disfigure and cripple, too, but killing is still their marquee attraction. Ace wasn't cute or smart or talented, but he was about to become the most famous entertainer in America. As his mind went black and the firearms roared in his hands he savored the confusion of those around him. Soon their instincts for self-preservation would kick in, but for now they hadn't yet processed that wounding of the hive that only a mass shooting can inspire.

Preternaturally calm, the voices in his head drowned out by gunfire and screaming, he attained a state of heightened consciousness and glimpsed eternity. *Here lies Ace Minarini, singer for the Dunderhearts; never nominated, but now and forever entwined with the Golden Calf Awards via public execution broadcast live.* Ace had never cared about money or fame, he just wanted to be in a band, quit his job and fuck Nina West. Now he'd lost everything and somebody, no everybody, had to pay.

And who among us hasn't thirsted to end the life of another, to extract one's own brand of justice when the universe won't play along? What man tormented hasn't longed to lay his tormentors low, what woman scorned hasn't dreamed of eviscerating her scorners? Only the tame and small of spirit. *(Author's Note: I'd like to kill anyone who didn't buy this book.)*

We can't always get what we want, that's true, but we can always ruin things. It's as easy as shouting down a campus speaker, reviewing a family owned restaurant with a single star or strangling kittens on a lonely country road; we find grim solace in these little puffs of schadenfreude that always seem to pass too quickly. With enough ordnance though, one individual can ruin multiple lives in an instant while still pulling in huge ratings among the coveted eighteen-to-thirty-five-year-old demographic.

"Vengeance is mine," sayeth the Lord. Even He has to get in on the act.

{56}

Nobody
But Me

†

BY THE TIME ACE HAD SAMPLED the depths of his popsicle box, hundreds of rounds had spewed forth from a MAC-11 automatic pistol that was almost certainly one bigger than the MAC-10. His control of the firearm was nonexistent, but by that point Ace didn't care. As slugs ricocheted around the hall he came to the realization that all humanity was the enemy, a question of Me vs. Them. And right about now, Me was winning.

For ratings, the Golden Calf Awards were winning, too. As soon as the ammunition had started flying the numbers began to climb. Of course, the folks at the Columbine Broadcasting Network System are human just like you and I. CBNS executives and board members alike looked on in horror as the scene unfolded across their channel. They saw the carnage and felt stirred to their marrow with compassion for the victims; their minds searched for workable ideas to end the epidemic of gun violence that had claimed so many innocents; and their souls wept for the common anguish of the entire human race in the face of this mindless destruction. A few seconds later, they got back to work. The show's technical director, ensconced in a booth at the back of the arena, toggled expertly between bleeding corpses, injured artistes and horrified bystanders. Fleeing spectators caused a bottleneck at the exits, effectively blocking armed security personnel from entering the main hall. Meanwhile, unsure where the shots had actually come from, much of the backstage crew had streamed onto the stage adding to the confusion and the body count as bullets continued to fly.

Birdie, still clutching Bella tight, attempted to rise to his feet, but the stampede onstage pinned him to the ground on top of her instead. Frantically he tried to rise, as Bella feebly squirmed at the bottom of the scrum. He could almost feel the will to live oozing out of her as he heaved upward with all of his might, but to no avail. After the longest twelve seconds of his life he managed to find his footing, losing his woman in the effort. As the crowd swept him along, Bella finally got her fondest wish and ceased to be, her supine form covered in dozens of desperate feet scrambling to find an exit.

Brian Kornfelter, eyes streaming with tears, caught site of Ace's profile and the gun barking fire in his hand. Buffeted forward by the crowd he fought his way toward the gunman, finally getting his hands around Ace's neck and squeezing for all he was worth. Ace continued firing as an off-duty LA policeman, believing that Birdie was the shooter, put two slugs squarely through his forehead. The introspective Dunderheart died much as he had lived, unknown and untalented, but also very much in love. In the Rock & Roll game you can call that a victory. As Birdie fell, Ace rose again shooting the cop between the eyes and screaming-

"Nobody kills this band but me!"

In the entertainment industry success breeds success, even as it traffics in disaster. Li'l Maple suffered a punctured lung in the attack, but it actually improved his singing voice and gave him something to rap about. Duchesse, suffering a massive chest wound, underwent a double mastectomy, eventually becoming honorary spokesperson for the Breast Cancer Awareness Fund. The following year, the GCA's introduced the *Dr. Gideon Balzfyre Encouraging Young Artists* award as well as the *Bella DuBois Triumph Over Adversity* award to its roster. The less famous victims simply died.

{57}

Nothing
Left To Prove

✝

THROUGHOUT THE MASSACRE, NINA STOOD her ground
stage right with Dr. Lukas Cosgrove by her side. A week ago, she
would have sworn that the Dunderhearts would never come within a
mile of the Golden Calf Awards. Now Ace was the star of the show.
She admired the look of elation on his face as he blasted away at
the crowd, it was more attractive than his usual angry scowl and
way better than listening to his music. He seemed happy and Nina
wanted him happy, so she'd never have to see him again.

Police and security got nearer to the action, but the crush of
bodies onstage and Ace's manic movements as he fired still prevented
them from shooting at the shooter without harming the crowd
around him. Ace could sense that his fifteen minutes were almost up.
With nothing left to prove he reached into the box and pulled out
three Vietnam era hand grenades, pulling the pins with his teeth and
tossing them in the direction of anything in a blue uniform. The addition of explosives to the bloodbath brought a new level of urgency to
the human stampede. Ace whirled around still pumping slugs into the
crowd as he caught site of Nina in the wings looking bored. Thinking
her a hallucination, he continued firing in all directions while instinctively making his way toward her.

Lance Middleton, sensing the perfect moment to save the day, leaned
over and kissed Nina, infuriating Ace as he tossed two more grenades

at the orchestra pit. Striding through the throng and removing a scalpel from his inside pocket, he deftly threw it at Ace piercing his left eyeball. Ace, too far gone to succumb to pain, continued firing, the surgical instrument hanging lasciviously from his face.

By now all of the rival networks were rebroadcasting Columbine Broadcasting's signal as breaking news. This infuriated the CBNS legal department, many of whom had been channel surfing and dreaming of billable hours. Mass carnage was bad, of course, but copyright infringement took things to a whole other level. Hijacking another network's signal and rebroadcasting it was tantamount to flinging dung at the Sistine Chapel or dubbing *Seinfeld* reruns into Arabic. An array of communications satellites located above the Earth's atmosphere relayed messages at top speed from CBNS' General Counsel to the CEO, to the director of the Golden Calf Awards and finally to Marissa Turnbull, Chief Technical Officer at Columbine Broadcasting.

Instructed to thwart the competition by scrambling the televised signal except to Columbine affiliates, Turnbull engaged the CBSN website as a backup in case transmission was compromised. Trying above all else to maintain the exclusive, she managed instead to transmit that signal live across the internet where it quickly took on a life of its own on the dark web. Between the actual broadcast and all of these other sources the 2020 GCA's quickly became the most watched live event in history, featuring a story line no film director would have ever dared choreograph. Representatives of Ford Motor Company, Pepsi Cola, Doritos and Exxon-Mobil, mortified by the lack of advertising displayed during the massacre, began drafting angry letters demanding restitution.

The image of Ace, scalpel in eye socket, ice cream box full of ammo around his neck, groping toward Lance Middleton bent on revenge was worth the price of admission for Nina West. It didn't escape her swollen ego that the two men who had inflicted the most harm so far were both in love with her. She wondered fleetingly if a three way would be out of the question.

In this corner, Dr. Lukas Cosgrove: rich, suave, handsome, famous, imaginary. He had maimed her psychotic ex-boyfriend at twenty paces and still his pants held their crease. In that corner, Ace Minarini: young, dumb, deranged and sporting an ever growing body count. He couldn't sing or dance, but he was responsible for a bloodbath that a good percentage of the Earth's inhabitants would wind up viewing from the comfort of their electronic devices. If that wasn't Rock & Roll then nothing was.

By this time, the police had regrouped and the throng onstage had cleared some, creating room to maneuver. While still careful to avoid bystanders, they began aiming at Ace and he took lead to the left ankle and shoulder that made him wince with pain. Yanking the blade from his eye, he made a desperate lunge for Cosgrove who lunged right back at him; this heroic action drove the sharpened metal tip of the scalpel deep into his heart and ended his fictional medical career for good.

"That's for kissing Nina," Ace said *sotto voce*, as they tumbled to the floor.

Dr. Lukas Cosgrove had attended Johns Hopkins Medical School and interned at the prestigious Mayo Clinic before transferring to *Doctor's Hospice* weekdays at 10:00 a.m. / 9:00 a.m. Central Time. But even with his fabricated talent and experience, he could not save himself. In one short evening, Lance Middleton had fallen in love and been murdered on national TV. A more fitting arc for a daytime actor would be hard to imagine, even without a writer's strike.

Ace rose painfully from the ground, guns blazing in a fresh fusillade that ended the lives of LAPD Officers Pete Nolan and Jesus "Chuy" Jimenez. Two more grenades chased their reinforcements under seats and into the aisles as they attempted to get a clear shot at the shooter. Another bullet grazed his side and his face contorted with pain, but without remorse. Ace Minarini was all in. The voices in his head had ceased, a performer's need for recognition finally realized beyond his wildest dreams. He was high on cocaine, permanently so, and police and security seemed powerless to stop him. Best of all, Nina West had witnessed his triumph. As she promenaded across the stage toward him he felt jubilant enough for them both, like Elvis and Priscilla entombed in bacon and peanut butter forever more.

Nina had seen all she needed to see. The sight of her throw away boyfriend destroying her make believe husband had turned her on so much that moistened panties were riding up her loins like waxed dental floss. Still, Ace would have to pay; not for the senseless terror he had inflicted on the masses, not even for his unforgivable lack of talent, but for detonating Nina's suburban dream of perfect romance with her very own television doctor.

{58}

Nina West
Iconic Legend

†

THE CAMERA PANNED FROM ACE to the cute but determined figure in short skirt and high boots who strode toward him fearlessly, her pale face expressing nothing. Ace hoped that before his life ended he could kiss her just one more time. The light caught the part in her hair as she pulled to within two feet of the gunman and in one swift motion placed a sassy white Gucci between his legs. Ace felt the pain of rejection psychically first, then the physical indignation of a boot to the groin. He fell to his knees as a bullet whizzed through the air where his head should have been. In spite of herself, Nina had saved his worthless hide once again.

Kneeling before her now, his head inches from her dewy cleft, he caught a hint of lavender and the essence of Dr. Lukas Cosgrove. The light went out behind his eyes then, the buzz evacuating his brain. With absolute clarity he saw the obscenity of himself: murderer, misanthrope, monster. Worst of all, he couldn't sing. Raising his left hand over his head and placing the gun in his mouth, his very last bullet in the chamber, Ace pulled the trigger that broke up the Dunderhearts for good.

Nina West, covered in the blood of a mass killer, strode to the center of the spotlight and looked out across the half empty auditorium. Corpses scattered along the aisles, in front of the stage, even in the catwalks above told a tale of senseless barbarity. A hush had enveloped the battered crowd, discombobulated but trained always to look toward the stage for a voice to guide them. Nina thought-

"Music can't be very difficult if these idiots make it."

Some moments are made for quiet contemplation, others for definitive action and some are just meant to be savored. This moment was made for TV. The instant that Nina opened her mouth to sing every bird in the sky quit its chirping, every human eye fixated on her. The sound commenced, somewhat quavering at first yet invulnerable, the digestif to a dinner of death. Her voice, untrained untamed, lit up the room-

Me and my shadow, Strolling down the avenue
Me and my shadow, not a soul to tell our troubles to
And when it's twelve o' clock, we climb the Stairs
We never knock, 'cause nobody's there
Just me and my shadow
All alone and feeling blue...

As the hushed room began to awaken the sound of this solitary performer cheered them in the depths of their despair. With each note Nina's voice gathered strength and clarity, supreme self-confidence asserting itself among the ruins. Like Shirley Temple in Vampira makeup she stepped out of the maw of madness and into the desolate heart of a new generation. Emergency medical personnel now filled the hall as phalanxes of armed police charged in, but everyone, no matter the importance of their mission, paused to drink in that relief that only a melodious human voice can provide. Even the afflicted, the injured and the deceased were transported for a moment. As the cameras zoomed in closer uncountable Ninas multiplied; Nina West, North, East and South spanned the globe and a legend was born.

Modern music is a cruel joke perpetrated on sheep-like consumers groping in the dark for a culture they cannot create themselves. And that's putting it politely. Forgotten for almost a century *Me and My Shadow* still spoke volumes across the years. It told of loneliness and longing, of hope and resignation and that agony that comes from truly knowing oneself. Had there been a producer or a session musician, a computer program or a piece of software to ruin it you might not be reading this now, but fate smiled and Nina was left in glorious solitude to ululate her ancient anthem up toward the ozone layer.

She only remembered the chorus part so she did it twice and by the time she had finished, to thunderous applause, Nina West had graduated from small town trickster to worldwide phenomenon. Her performance over, the first real effort she'd put into anything since a particularly revealing Show and Tell in the third grade, she found herself musing-

"How late is the In-N-Out drive-thru open? I'm starving."

Nina had revealed the cracks in commercial music's glittery façade to a world that didn't yet know what it needed to hear. Somehow, the current scene with its air tight production values and interchangeable stars seemed thoroughly tapped out. Even Ace was already yesterday's news, he had lived on the edge, but died on his knees. In one magical televised moment Nina had vaulted beyond them all with no management, no record label, no promotion and no rehearsal; she didn't even *like* music. Forever after they would eat her dust, the whole lot of them reduced to a cast of singing monkeys schooled by an organ grinder who cared even less than they did.

Without warning, a familiar head poked from between her legs. Easy, the last of the Dunderhearts, had raised her up on his shoulders for a slow trek off stage and up the center aisle, satellite transmission recording every triumphant moment until they disappeared from the camera's sight. When they reached the lobby, Easy set her down gently and disappeared into the night, his future unknown, but the entire parking lot at his feet. Outside the arena a blood-spattered red carpet led to a white limousine. The back door opened suggestively and Nina slipped inside.

"You've come a long way from Highland Falls, young lady, and you're going to need some representation. You're already a star, I think I can make you a very wealthy one."

Nina considered the man before her, the lights and sirens surrounding them, the onrush of media, photographers, security and sycophants. With the reverence of the event now shattered, she balled up her small right fist and punched Grubmann squarely in the eye just as hard as she could. Now he would truly see stars. A long moment passed while Nina reflected on the first moon landing and the Peloponnesian War. As Ross Grubmann regained consciousness he heard her say, "That sounds peachy to me." ❦

ABOUT THE AUTHOR

Blag Dahlia is a rock legend. Founder of seminal punk band the Dwarves, he has been performing and recording independent music across the globe for over four decades. His work has been released by some of the most influential independent labels and has appeared in dozens of feature films and hundreds of television shows, skate videos and multimedia projects. Blag cohosted the podcast *Radio Like You Want* and the advice show *We Got Issues* that ran on San Francisco's esteemed KFOG. As a writer of fiction, Dahlia has penned two previous works: *Nina*, the story of a teenage sociopath told with a mixture of humor, sex, minimalism and more sex; and *Armed to the Teeth with Lipstick*, an experimental word salad with illustrations by Mad Marc Rude.

ACKNOWLEDGEMENTS

Thanks to Phil and Kris Cafaro for editorial love and support; Pamela Holm for her tireless efforts to find a publisher for me; Zoe Lacchei for her cover illustration; Dana Collins for his designs and advice; and to my friends the Dwarves, long may they reign.

Thank you to the composers of these songs in the Public Domain:
"Motherless Child" (Traditional)
"Me and My Shadow" (Dreyer/Rose)